Fancy White Trash

Fancy White Trash

Marjetta Geerling

Viking

Viking

Published by Penguin Group

Penguin Group (USA) Inc., 345 Hudson Street, New York, New York 10014, U.S.A.

Penguin Group (Canada), 90 Eglinton Avenue East, Suite 700, Toronto, Ontario, Canada M4P 2Y3
(a division of Pearson Penguin Canada Inc.)

Penguin Books Ltd, 80 Strand, London WC2R 0RL, England

Penguin Ireland, 25 St Stephen's Green, Dublin 2, Ireland (a division of Penguin Books Ltd)

Penguin Group (Australia), 250 Camberwell Road, Camberwell, Victoria 3124, Australia
(a division of Pearson Australia Group Pty Ltd)

Penguin Books India Pvt Ltd, 11 Community Centre, Panchsheel Park, New Delhi – 110 017, India

Penguin Group (NZ), 67 Apollo Drive, Rosedale, North Shore 0632, New Zealand
(a division of Pearson New Zealand Ltd.)

Penguin Books (South Africa) (Pty) Ltd, 24 Sturdee Avenue, Rosebank, Johannesburg 2196,
South Africa

Penguin Books Ltd, Registered Offices: 80 Strand, London WC2R 0RL, England

First published in 2008 by Viking, a member of Penguin Group (USA) Inc.

10 9 8 7 6 5 4 3 2 1

LIBRARY OF CONGRESS CATALOGING-IN-PUBLICATION DATA

Geerling, Marjetta.

Fancy white trash / by Marjetta Geerling.

p. cm.

Summary: Fifteen-year-old Abby Savage hopes that her five rules for falling in love will keep her
from making the same mistakes as her mother and two older sisters—all unwed mothers who have
slept with the same man, among others—while she also tries to help her best friend Cody admit
that he is gay, and decide how she really feels about Cody's older brother, Jackson.

ISBN 978-0-670-01082-0 (hardcover)

[1. Family problems—Fiction. 2. Interpersonal relations—Fiction. 3. Homosexuality—Fiction.
4. Best friends—Fiction. 5. Friendship—Fiction. 6. Arizona—Fiction.] I. Title.

PZ7.G25842Fan 2008   [Fic]—dc22   2007038214

Printed in U.S.A.   Set in Berkeley   Book design by Nancy Brennan

This book is dedicated to my sisters,
Debbie Jones and Joni Combs,
because we know that truth is much
stranger than fiction.

And

In memory of our mother,
Diana Geerling,
who was practically perfect in every way.

Fancy White Trash

Chapter ♥ 1

There are five rules for falling in love. I figured them out from watching my sisters and a lot of daytime television. There's wisdom in soap operas, especially the ones that have been around longer than most of us have been alive. I've paid attention, taken notes, and pooled all this accumulated knowledge into what I like to call my One True Love Plan.

Don't laugh. Believe me, if you'd watched two older, boy-crazy sisters totally bungle their love lives, you'd have a plan, too. If your mom divorced your dad then married him again, then left him again, and then married your sister's guitar instructor, you'd be extra careful about commitments. If your eighteen-year-old sister, only three years older than you, was pregnant with your oldest sister's ex-boyfriend's baby, you'd be saving it for Mr. Right. And you'd know that Mr. Right had not already dated one of your sisters.

That's why Rule #1 is Find Someone New. But at Union High, it is impossible to Find Someone New. We have all been together since our moms gave birth to us at the Cottonwood Medical Center. Because back then, there was only one hospital in Cottonwood, Arizona, like there was only one elementary school, one middle school, one movie theater . . . you get the picture.

By ninth grade, everyone had already dated everyone else—or if they hadn't, there was a real good reason. Like Carolyn Schmitz's weird, drooly laugh or Lucas Fielding's lazy eye. Or like me, who was Not Into Boys after seeing exactly what giving birth looks like, thanks to my oldest sister's insistence that we all be present for the "miracle" of her daughter Hannah's delivery.

My sisters also went to Union High, but although they're both past their eighteenth birthdays now, they did not go to any of the best colleges. Or any college, for that matter. Shelby, the oldest at twenty-one and Hannah's mom, got married the week after graduation and divorced by that Christmas. Super-pregnant Kaitlyn is a senior, again. Me, I'm cruising into sophomore year with my academic butt covered and my One True Love Plan waiting to be deployed.

That's a lot of people in not a lot of living space. Mom keeps saying we're moving to one of those big mansions in Scottsdale, but I'm not too worried about being forced to relocate. Although her new hubby is supposed to help with expenses, she still can barely pay the mortgage on our fake adobe five-girl, one-guy, one-bathroom house.

"Abby, phone!" Kait yells, even though she is in the same room, our room, and can see perfectly well that I'm right here. Eight months of pregnancy have not improved her personality, but she must be in a good mood because usually she hangs up on whoever asks for me.

I dog-ear the page I'm reading in *Soap Digest* and lunge for the phone which is, as always, on Kait's side of the room. Kait's idea of decorating is to bring home old movie posters from Blockbuster, where she works, which wouldn't be so bad if she had decent taste in movies. But no, she's got a thing for romantic comedies, especially old ones, so our room is an homage to Meg Ryan and Drew Barrymore. Hello, *You've Got Mail* and *Home Fries.* Kindly stay on your side of the room.

I grab the phone from Kait and flop back on my twin bed. The metal frame screeches in protest.

"Abigail Elizabeth Savage, we still on for our back-to-school shopping extravaganza tomorrow?" It's Cody Jennings, my next-door neighbor, who likes to stress the importance of something by using my full name.

Before you get your hopes up, let me tell you that this is not one of those situations where the girl goes out with the empty-headed jock only to realize that her soul mate was living next door to her all along. Cody is gay. He hasn't told me—or anyone—yet, but I know. When you've been best friends with a guy your whole life, it's pretty easy to figure out.

"Of course we're still on. Did you think I'd forget in the less than"—I check my *Little Mermaid* alarm clock for the time—"two hours since we talked about it? It's not like I have amnesia." Amnesia is a popular disease on daytime television. Everyone gets it at least once in their lives.

"First thing in the morning, right? Because you know I like to be there when the stores open."

"A.M. is no problem for me. The baby starts screaming early."

"Do not bring the baby," Cody says.

He isn't being paranoid. Shelby has dumped the baby on us many times. That is why Rule #2 is No Baggage from Past Relationships Allowed, and that definitely includes kids. It also includes psycho exes (Shelby has two) and pets. Kait's first boyfriend's snake is still living in our house—literally. Sometimes I think I hear it in the walls.

"Don't worry. I'm not babysitting tomorrow." The baby, three-year-old Hannah, is really not so bad, but she's not my kid—a concept Shelby has difficulty grasping.

"You're so good with her," Shelby always cajoles, which is actually her way of saying that she has a date that night. Shelby takes after our mom, who is, if not movie-star gorgeous, more beautiful than most women, with her shiny black hair and unusually light blue eyes. I have the same coloring but whack my hair off in uneven layers so I won't be mistaken for one of "those Savage girls."

"Hello?" Cody is impatient, which means I have spaced out. Thinking about my slutty sisters always sidetracks me. "I asked who's driving us."

This part he will not like. "My mom."

I can actually hear his teeth grinding through the phone. "You can't get anyone else?"

"What do you think? If you would hurry up and turn sixteen, we wouldn't have to risk our lives this way." Cody is three months older than I am, so he'll get his license before me, and also a car. I will not be getting a car.

"I'm working on it. You think I'm not dreaming about the day we can hop in my convertible and hit the mall whenever we want?" Cody has been lobbying hard for the new Sebring but will be happy if he scores a used one. If not that, I'm pretty sure anything with wheels will do.

"What should I wear?" I ask him, not because he's gay, but because he's obsessive. Anal. Practically OCD. Which means he has strong opinions about how *everything* should be just *so*, especially when it comes to appearance. Nothing upsets him more than an outfit gone wrong. That's why it's easier for me to ask his opinion beforehand than to have to change everything once he sees me.

"You should wear the red tank so the bloodstains won't be as noticeable when the paramedics pry our dead bodies out of the remains of your mom's latest traffic accident." Car accidents are very popular on soap operas. They're also quite common in my family, at least when my mom is driving.

I think she has some kind of spatial-distortion/color-blindness learning disability, but she won't admit it. The whole town knows my mom's red "vintage" Mercedes sedan with the duct-taped plastic passenger-side window. No one parks next to her in the parking lots; no one demands right-of-way at four-way stops.

I hear the Mercedes pull into the drive. It's not sounding too good, like maybe it has pneumonia. *Hhhfft, hhhftt.* Doesn't bode well for our shopping trip tomorrow. Every part on that car costs $500 to replace, so a lot of repairs get postponed. Or overlooked altogether. When the rear bumper fell off, Mom said, "I think the car looks better without that thing anyway." It's got to be the white-trashiest Mercedes-Benz in the world.

"Bad news," I say into the phone, about to warn Cody that

our trip may be off due to chronic car disease, but I'm interrupted when the front door slams against the wall. Uh-oh, dramatic entrance. Something's definitely up.

"Everyone!" my mom shrills at the top of her lungs. The Guitar Player comes running. Kait lurches to her feet, easily distracted from painting her fingernails Totally Tangerine, a completely hideous color if you ask me—which no one has, so I don't point out how it makes her fingers look stubby. I stay stretched out on my bed and contemplate the many hairstyles of Meg and Drew.

I hear whooping and what sounds like the Guitar Player jumping up and down on the wood floors in his motorcycle boots. He has a name, but to me he'll always be the Guitar Player, just like Dad will always be Dad.

"Pregnant?" Shelby shrieks. She's been living with us since the divorce. Which was three years ago. Some people should get their own lives, not hang around hogging all the bathroom time.

"Pregnant?" Cody echoes on the phone. "Who, Shelby?" Whether he's heard it through the phone or through the window, it's hard to tell.

"Gotta go." I hoist myself upright. "I'll call you back with the pedigree, but I think it's my mom."

"Your mom? I can't—" I hang up on him. I can't believe it, either. Didn't she get her tubes tied? Who has four kids nowadays? Who has their fourth kid fifteen years after the third?

Everyone is crammed into the kitchen when I get there. Although Kait shares our dark hair, she always looks the odd one out, taking after our dad with her brown eyes and stockier body. She's the shortest, too, and since she's not the youngest, that infuriates her. Of course, her pregnancy hormones make it so she is always furious lately. Or crying. It's difficult to predict which way she'll go—throwing stuff or sobbing—so I mostly try to stay out of her way.

Kait sits at our big kitchen table with the cherries-in-a-bowl-patterned plastic tablecloth—easier than fabric for wiping up all of Hannah's spills—with her head in her hands. She's biting her lip so hard, I'm afraid it might bleed. Mom and the Guitar Player are also at the table, with Hannah playing on the floor at their feet. Shelby stands apart, in front of the stainless-steel sink, with the bright sun from the window backlighting her dramatically and bringing out the cinnamon highlights she recently added to her hair.

I fold my own long body into one of the kitchen chairs. It is older than I am and creaks under my weight. I make a mental note to remember to Super Glue the crossbars back in place. You'd think the Guitar Player, as the official and only man of the house for two months now, would be in charge of the manly chores like taking out the trash and Super Gluing things together. But apparently he's too busy getting my mom pregnant.

"It's too early to tell"—my mom pats her flat belly—"but I just know it's a boy." That's what she said about me and Hannah, too. I bet she pops out another girl. We already know Kait's baby is a girl. Our family should buy stock in Always brand products.

"When?" I ask the only sensible question while Shelby brings up whether Connor or Dylan is a better name for a boy.

It's not like I'm suspicious or anything, but Mom's figure is as slim as ever.

Kait lumbers to her feet, one hand under her tremendous belly, the other on the small of her back. "I'll be in my room," she says so softly I almost don't hear. Her lip *is* bleeding. She wipes at it with a fist and, eyes down, leaves the room.

"He may be a Valentine baby!" Mom announces once Kait is out of the kitchen, showing her usual amount of sensitivity—zero. She actually dances with excitement, a little two-steppy bounce that calls attention to the way her breasts fill out her tube top.

Math isn't my best subject, but even I can count backwards from nine. Mom must've conceived in May—the same month she and the Guitar Player tied the knot—making her almost three months pregnant now.

The Guitar Player looks pleased. So does Mom. She has no shame, marrying a guy half her age (that would be Shelby's age) and proceeding to get knocked up right away. Although, I hate to admit, soap operas also favor pregnancies as a way of cementing new relationships. I should've expected this, but I didn't.

I ask the next logistics question. "Where will we put the new baby?" We are already packed to the rafters when it comes to room occupancy. I can't imagine where another crib and all the other baby stuff can possibly fit.

"He'll be in our room, of course," Mom says, like that's the end of it. Like the baby won't grow up and need a toddler bed, then a regular bed, closet space, or time in the bathroom.

"I'll need to clear out a few things first, but I'm sure it'll work out. We'll get some of those walkie-talkie things so we can hear when he wakes up no matter where we are in the house. What're they called?"

"Baby monitors," Shelby supplies. She should know, since it was Mom who said we didn't have money for such high-tech gadgets when Hannah was born. Guess things'll be different with this baby. *His* baby. I glare in the general direction of the Guitar Player. Why doesn't he bring up something practical, like getting a combo dresser/changing table, instead of standing there with that stupid grin on his face?

Mom tilts her head and smiles. "Oh, I'm so excited. Let's go to Target right now! Abs, have you seen my keys?"

Like I'm the keeper of lost things. Except, I do know where they are. Instead of telling her, I say, "Do you really think you should be driving in your condition? Isn't it a little dangerous, considering . . ." I trail off, because everyone knows what I mean.

She starts to protest, but the Guitar Player agrees with me for once.

"Maybe you should take it easy for a while," he says.

"Steve, please, I drove with all my other pregnancies." Steve is the Guitar Player's real name.

"Not with my baby," he says, and Mom gives him a sharp look. A look I know well. The honeymoon is over. Even though they didn't go anywhere after their quickie marriage last May, they did enjoy a little over two months of disgusting togetherness.

The Guitar Player cradles her hand in his. He doesn't know it's over. "Come on, honey, I'll be your chauffeur. Won't that be fancy?"

Fancy White Trash, that's us all right.

"What about the mall tomorrow? You gonna drive then, too?" I look over the Guitar Player's shoulder. I never address him directly.

"Sure, Mona and I will need to pick up some other things for the baby. Right, honey?"

I want to point out that we have three tons of baby crap stored in the garage, but then I realize Kait's baby will need that stuff. We don't have two of everything.

I smile brightly and say, "Good point!"

Mom chews her lip and I say how Cody's coming, too. We all look at Shelby, who has been quiet—too quiet—through this whole conversation.

Once all eyes are on her, she flips back her waist-length hair and rubs her own stomach. "I was waiting until I was sure, but . . ." She looks at us expectantly.

She has got to be kidding. Mom shoots me a look, and I realize I've groaned out loud.

Shelby bursts into tears. "You always think the worst of me, Abby."

"Who's the dad?" I ask the question on everyone's mind.

Shelby's eyes dart toward the Guitar Player and away. Mom gasps.

"No, no!" Shelby puts a protective hand over her stomach.

But I saw the Guitar Player pale, and I know it wasn't that long ago that he and Shelby were doing it. Oh God, can it be true? Would it take Shelby four months to notice she's pregnant?

Mom turns to the Guitar Player. "Steve?" Her face looks like it will collapse any minute.

"Let's have a pig roast!" the Guitar Player yells too loudly, fiddling nervously with one of the fake diamond studs in his ear. "What a lot to celebrate!" He spent his formative years in Miami, where, apparently, it's just not a celebration without a dead pig. He digs into his jeans for the keys. "Tonight! Everyone call somebody to come over. I'll be back with supplies in no time."

I don't know where he finds whole dead pigs in this town. I do know Cody is going to die when I tell him. Three babies on the way, all with the same dad. Obviously, no one in my family has contemplated the wisdom of Rule #1, Find Someone New, because they're all on the recycling program.

That's right, the Guitar Player "dated" Kait for about two weeks before he dumped her for Shelby. Since his idea of dating has less to do with romantic dinners and getaways to the river and more to do with getting the women in my family naked, it's not too surprising someone turned up pregnant. But three? Could my family be more embarrassing?

Chapter 2

"No, no, no!" Shelby has to scream to get everyone refocused on her. "I'm not pregnant! I signed up to be an egg donor. You can make beaucoup bucks harvesting eggs."

Beaucoup is a fancy white trash word for "a lot." I think it's French or something. The Guitar Player looks beaucoup relieved. Mom dabs at her eyes. Shelby laughs while I stand by, struck dumb by the idea of someone actually wanting Shelby's genetic material. Sure, she's beautiful but . . .

That leads us directly to Rule #3 in the One True Love Plan: Looks Aren't Everything. Take the classic soap, *Moments of Our Lives*, as an example. Between their First Loves coming back from the dead the same day they are marrying the Loves of Their Lives and never being sure who the father of their child is, *Moments* characters have one love crisis after another.

It's clear to me that the problem is they are all too good-looking. Sure, it's why the show's been on the air for over twenty years, but it's like having dessert for every meal of the day. At first, you think red-velvet cake for dinner is a great idea, but after a few years, all you want is a nice crispy salad or a side of french fries. I'm not saying you have to eat dog food here—even I am not going to date Lucas Fielding—but to fall in love, you need someone who is not all sugary sweetness.

Shelby is pure sugar. I'm surprised her fake tears don't melt grooves in her cheeks. "I won't know for sure if they'll take my eggs until all the donor-screening tests come back, but everyone's been harping on me to get a better-paying job. I thought you'd be happy."

The Guitar Player inches closer and closer to the side door, the one that leads to the driveway and his escape vehicle. "Like I said, lots to celebrate. I'll be back in a few."

Mom looks fine now, but I haven't forgotten that for a second, the Guitar Player thought what I thought. Which means maybe it wasn't as long ago as everyone thinks since he and Shelby called it quits. It wouldn't surprise me. The Guitar Player is a scrumptious-looking man. Dirty-blond hair with sun-streaked highlights and intense almost-black eyes, always in faded jeans that cup his amazingly tight butt. He knows how to work the wannabe-rock-star image, but like I said, Looks Aren't Everything.

"I'm going next door," I announce, unfolding from my chair and stretching. I tug at my jeans and pull down my pink T-shirt so my belly button doesn't show. "Congrats, Mom. And Shelby."

Shelby keeps her place at the big table, tracing one of the faded cherries on the tablecloth with a long Red Dazzle nail. Her eyes have dried up. I guess the good thing about fake tears is you can turn them on and off at will. Hannah bangs away happily at the table legs with a spoon she must've found under there.

"Are you really happy for me, Abby?" Mom links her arm through mine and walks with me to the front door. We pass the collage of school pictures taped to the wall. Shelby first, then Kait, then me. Year after year, marching down the hallway.

"This new baby is like starting over," Mom says. "It's so important to Steve, but to tell you the truth, I had a minor panic attack when the doctor told me today. It's been a long time since you were in diapers."

"Hannah's kept us all in practice. Don't worry, Mom, you'll be fine." It's the baby I'm worried about. As a parent, Mom has her shortcomings. Like forgetting me at the grocery store when I was three. I sat in the cart in the frozen-food section for almost an hour before someone wheeled me to the manager. Luckily, she also left her purse, so they were able to contact her right away.

"You'll help out, won't you?" Mom asks. "I won't be able to do this without the support of my girls."

Ha! Like she was really supporting her girls when she started sleeping with the Guitar Player. Like she was thinking of her daughters when she married him at the courthouse and didn't invite any of us to the ceremony. This is so *Veterans' Hospital*, I expect to hear theme music pipe in from above at any moment.

"I could be really helpful running errands for you in my own car." I am supposed to share Kait's car when I turn sixteen. Which means I will have to get a job so I can help pay the insurance for a car that she will never let me drive. Maybe this baby can be my ticket to vehicular freedom.

"You're so funny." Mom laughs, and she looks young to me. Too young to be anyone's mom. It's easy to see why her boss at the advertising agency keeps her around even though she's hopeless with computers.

I don't reply, open the door, and walk the fifty-eight paces to Cody's. He is waiting for me on the enclosed front porch. At last, a sane person!

"Tell me everything." He pats the seat next to him on the rocker. His hazel eyes are bright with interest. "Everything."

I do, and he nods his head like this is all totally believable and normal. That's why we're best friends. He knows my crazy family and likes me anyway.

"It all sounds so *Savage*," he says. He likes to make jokes like this ever since he found out in second grade that *savage* has another meaning besides being my last name. "I mean, isn't your mom kind of old to be having another baby?"

"She's only thirty-seven," I reply, although come to think of it, that is pretty ancient. "But she *thinks* she's still nineteen. Like we need another teen mother at our house."

"Maybe it won't be so bad," Cody, far less cynical than I am when it comes to my family, says. "New marriage, new baby, new life. This could be your mom's opportunity to do things right."

Oh, how I wish it were true. "For her to make things right, she'd have to admit to doing something *wrong*. We both know that's not Mona's style. I'm afraid this baby is doomed, like the rest of us Savage girls."

"You didn't turn out so bad." Cody sets the porch swing to rocking with a push of his foot. "And you can watch over the baby, kind of like you already do for Hannah. You'll be, like, the Fairy Godmother of Normalness."

"Right, my dream has always been to raise other people's babies."

"Better than raising your own."

"So true." A definite lesson I've learned from my sisters is that teen pregnancy is not pretty. "I'm going to break family tradition and make it to graduation without getting knocked up. What do you think of that?"

Cody grins. "Simple yet so profound. You'll be a great big sis with wisdom like that to share."

I hope he's right. Because I don't have a lot of faith that anyone else is going to be looking out for this kid. But all we can really do, I guess, is wait and see.

"Cody, we need to go." His mom joins us on the porch, all sunny in her head-to-toe yellow dress and matching sandals. "Hi, Abby. What's new with you?"

"Nothing, Barbara, but thanks for asking." I smile.

Cody pulls a crumpled paper out of his pocket and consults it. "His flight doesn't land for hours. Besides, I need to change."

"I don't want to get stuck in traffic." Barbara is such a worrier. "You know how it gets around the airport."

"Airport?" I ask.

"Yeah, Jackson's coming home. I told you, remember?" Cody stuffs the paper back in his pocket.

"Right. Hey, that reminds me. The Guitar Player is having another pig roast tonight. You guys should come."

"What's the occasion?" she asks.

Cody laughs and I shush him. Barbara is already not a big fan of my mom. No reason to add fuel to that fire.

"Just an end-of-summer thing." My voice squeaks at the end, always a sign that I'm lying, but she seems to buy it.

Barbara smiles wide and combs blonde bangs out of her eyes. "How lovely! We were planning a quiet little dinner for Jackson, but I know he'd love to catch up with you all. Can you believe it's been two months? I don't know what I'll do when he leaves for college."

"Yeah, yeah, yeah," Cody mumbles. "Jackson the wonderful, Jackson the magnificent."

Jackson, Cody's older brother. Jackson, who mentioned it every day for a month when I started wearing a bra. Jackson, who brought two friends to my eleventh birthday party and ate so much cake that I never got a piece. Jackson, Kait's ex-boyfriend and one-time suspected father of her child.

"He'll flip when he sees Kait," I say, imagining the look on Jackson's face when he encounters the Great White Blimp for the first time. "He is sooo lucky it's not his."

Barbara looks at me disapprovingly, but Cody cracks up.

"Sorry," I say to Barbara. "I should let you guys go. See you tonight?"

"I'll bring a macaroni salad," Barbara says.

See what I mean? Nice, normal family. Why can't I have one of those?

✳ ✳ ✳ ✳ ✳

Rule #4: Don't Need Him. Want him, like him, love him—
but never, ever need him. Case in point: my dad. Who is
sitting on the porch, next to the rickety bug zapper, nursing
his Bud Light. He's a handsome enough guy, with a decent job
as a salesman over at Chapman's Hardgoods, and is pretty
funny when he's drunk. Overall, not a bad catch.

Mom married him twice and she's never hurt for choices
when it comes to guys, so he's certainly matrimonial material. It's just that you can't count on him. Oh, he'll promise
you anything. A shiny new bike for your birthday, a complete
makeover at the mall when you turn thirteen, that he'll be at
the awards presentation when you are the first person in your
family to ever make honor roll. But you can't believe him. I
did, and was disappointed every time. I guess Mom felt the
same.

Now Dad is on wife number two, or three depending on
how you count it, and she is not funny when she's drunk. She
arrived at the pig roast already lit and has been hanging on the
Guitar Player ever since he broke out the acoustic and played
"Tears in Heaven" for her. She got all weepy and clingy, and
hasn't left his side since. Dad doesn't seem to notice, which is
probably another reason Mom divorced him.

"Daddy!" Hannah sees him from across the yard and
launches herself at my father. She has not grasped the com-
plexity of family relationships. All men are "Daddy."

"Pumpkin!" He catches her and kisses her cheek. "Pumpkin" used to be my special nickname.

The combined smell of electrocuted insects and beer makes me a bit light-headed. Dad swats at a fly that gets too close to his drink, misses, and knocks the bottle to the ground. Chuckling, he picks it up, wipes the mouth with the bottom of his not-so-clean blue shirt, and takes a swig.

Although the temperature's taken a dive since the afternoon, it's still hot enough that sweat glues my white tee with the climbing gray vines to my back. There's also a not-so-comfortable ring of perspiration under the waistband of my jean shorts. I grab a Bud from the red-and-white Igloo and park next to Dad and Hannah on the peeling wooden bench and take a long drink to cool off. Cody and his family aren't back from the airport yet, so I have no one to share my witty comments with. I settle for the beer and a handful of Cheetos.

"How's it going, Abby?" Dad asks. He bounces Hannah on his knee while she yells, "Go, horsey, go!" and slaps his leg. Her dark, bowl-cut hair flops up and down in time to her ride.

"The same." I stuff another Cheeto in my mouth. "You?"

He looks over where Wife Number Two/Three is currently sitting on the Guitar Player's lap. "Shevon wants a divorce."

"Bummer." I knock back a few swallows of beer. "What's it been, less than six months? You gonna try counseling or anything?"

He shrugs. "Naw, she can have the divorce. Can't cook worth beans anyways."

Dad's rules for falling in love are different from mine. I think they go something like 1. Female? 2. Breathing? 3. Cooks? And he's always so surprised when things don't go well.

"Maybe you can work it out," I say, because, sheesh people, isn't marriage supposed to mean something?

"Maybe," he agrees, and drains his beer. "Get me another, will you, Abs?"

I do, then wander away from the roasting pig and around the side of the house. There's a tree on the property line between my house and Cody's. We built a fort up there a million years ago, but it has mostly disintegrated. The steps are still nailed to the trunk, so I lift myself up to the first one and wrap my arms around the tree. My fingers dig into the bark.

I breathe in the tree, the dirt smell and dampness, and feel the tightness that was growing in my chest all night relax. I go up another step and another until I am high enough to scoot out onto the lowest bough. I wedge myself between the trunk and branch. Now, if only someone would bring me another beer.

"Lookin' for this?"

Cody holds up a can. Coke.

"You got some rum for that?" I ask, just to see him squirm.

"My mom's here. You know how she is." He braces a foot against the bottom of the tree. "But I can leave, you know, if you don't want it."

"Don't be so hasty," I say with a smile. "Come on and join me already."

Cody scrambles up the tree. I move over to make room, but even though he's not a big guy, it's a tight squeeze. He pops open the soda and hands it to me.

"Thanks. When'd you get here?"

"While you were having a personal moment with the tree. I decided to give you some privacy." He lays his head on my shoulder. "It sucks that we only have one more weekend of freedom. Can you believe school starts Monday?"

Cody hates school. Not like everybody hates school, in that won't-it-be-great-when-we're-seniors-and-can-finally-get-out-of-this-place? way. But in a real, physical, stomachache-in-the-mornings, please-Mom-I'm-begging-you-let-me-stay-home way. If I could, I'd homeschool him myself. He's plenty smart. It's the teasing that gets him.

"It'll be different," I tell him. "Now that Jackson's not on campus, everyone will stop comparing you two. We won't be freshmen. We'll be nice, boring, no-one-will-notice-us sophomores."

"You promise?"

I give him the last half of my Coke. "I promise."

"Cody and Abby sittin' in a tree, k-i-s-s-i-n-g!"

It's true that Cody and I once kissed in this very tree, but that was fourth grade and only one other person on the planet knows about that kiss.

"Shut up, Jack-Off." I use my nickname for Cody's brother without even looking down.

"First comes love, then comes marriage . . . oh, wait, you're one of those Savage girls. First comes love, then comes the baby, then comes the welfare check in the mail. . . ."

I chuck the empty soda can his way and bean him right on the forehead.

"Nice one," says Cody.

Jackson rubs his head like it actually hurt. "Nice to see you, too, Abs. Don't bother comin' down and givin' me a hug or anything. I've only been gone two months. You probably didn't even notice."

"I did, too. It was so much more pleasant without you."

"Get down here," he says.

I take off a shoe and throw it at him.

He ducks this time, and my flip-flop skids off his back. "Hey, now, no need to get violent. Just thought you two might like a beer?" He holds up a six-pack with one finger. Jackson has never been afraid to buck his parents when it comes to alcohol. Pretty smooth, sneaking that out of a party right under their noses. Hey, not everyone can have parents as understanding as mine.

"Why didn't you say so?" I clamber down the crumbling wooden steps. Cody's right behind me.

"Give us a hug first." Jackson holds the beers over my head. Although I'm not short, he's pushing six feet, so it's not exactly a fair contest. I jump and he lifts them higher.

"I'm not hugging you." I kick him with the ball of my bare foot. He yelps and too late shields his knee with both hands, dropping the beer.

Cody grabs the six-pack and I retrieve my shoe. "Run!" Cody shouts.

He takes off, avoids the party, which is mostly just our two families and a few neighbors spread out around the pig-pit, and runs for the back fence. It's not much of a fence, more a line in the sand than an actual barrier against the desert. Cody shoves aside a loose panel and slides through. I'm right behind him until I feel a tug on the back of my T-shirt.

"Let go, Jack-Off!" I lunge for the fence but get caught between the panels. Cody pulls on my arm, trying to help me through. Jackson grabs the back of my shirt, then gets a hand around my waist and hauls me back toward his side.

"Ow!" Cody apparently encounters some kind of wild desert plant. Saguaro cactus can be surprisingly pointy, and since they're protected by the state, they are everywhere. He lets go of my arm, and the force of Jackson's pull has me tumbling out onto his side of the fence.

"Got you." He pulls me against his chest for a hug. My mouth goes dry. "Missed you," he whispers into my ear.

Rule #5 of the One True Love Plan is Get Out of Town. Because if Jackson and I had run away together that first week of May, that once-in-a-lifetime week when I really, truly believed he was both my First Love and the Love of My Life, then maybe we could've made it.

On *Moments of Our Lives*, when the actress who played Candy wanted to leave the show, her character bought a sailboat and took off on a world cruise with the Love of Her Life. Later, both actors came back, their characters returned to town, and all hell broke loose again.

That's what it felt like, standing in the dark with Jackson's arms around me again. All hell was breaking loose in my body. I remembered too much about him, the feel of his chest under my hand, the steady *thump-thump* of his heart. For a crazy second, I wanted to reach up and kiss him, tell him how I'd missed him every day.

But it was too late for us. We hadn't run away, just kissed a lot and pretended to study for our final exams together. Then, instead of enjoying the prestige of dating a senior during graduation week and maybe getting invited to parties that freshmen only dream of going to, I'd had to deal with Mom and the Guitar Player announcing their engagement and Kait turning up pregnant. *Five months* pregnant, proving that peasant tops were not, in fact, coming back in style and that it wasn't depression eating that had added those extra pounds to her waistline.

Kait claimed the baby was the Guitar Player's, and I believed her until Shelby revealed—in the biggest Savage Family Blow-Out of the Century—that the baby could just as easily be Jackson's. I'd never even known Kait and Jackson had dated. When he didn't deny it, we were over.

Two weeks later, Jackson graduated and was off to Central America to build houses for the poor. He never even sent a postcard.

Finally, I push away from Jackson. "What, no slutty families to make your way through in Nicaragua?"

"Shut up, Abby, you know it wasn't like that."

"I do?"

"Fine." He slumps against the fence. "Have at me. You never got to say your piece, did you?"

Even in the dark, he is too beautiful. I can't look at him, the hard edge of his jaw and his deep blue eyes. His soft, white-blond hair hangs in his face.

"I have nothing to say to you." I push through the fence. Cody's waiting on the other side, open beer extended.

I take it and slug the whole thing back in three gulps.

"Everything okay?" he asks. "I thought you two could use a minute."

I shake my head because I really don't want to talk about it. "Beer me." I hold my hand out, and he gives me another.

He leads me farther into the desert. It is miles and miles to the next development. The cacti are dark shadows in the night. We find a relatively clear spot of sand and sit. Millions of stars sparkle above us.

"It's not over," Cody says, like it is a fact.

"It has to be."

"What if he really loves you?"

I perk up at this. Cody, after all, might know. "What do you think?"

He shrugs. "I'm just saying, what if?"

I am too old to play what-if games. I have my new One True Love Plan, and I'm going to make it work. Jackson is the anti–True Love. If I stick to my Rules, I'll be able to forget him in no time.

Chapter ♥ 3

By the time Cody and I get back to the pig roast, we've finished the six-pack. I keep looking back toward the fence, but Jackson doesn't come after us. We search the cooler for more Bud Light but only find wine coolers. I take a raspberry and give Cody a hard lemonade.

"My mom can't see me drinking." Cody thinks he's whispering, but it comes out too loud. He's such a lightweight.

I knock my bottle against his. "Cheers, bud, it's only lemonade."

He squints at the label. "You're so right."

We are not exactly stealthy as we settle onto a picnic bench beside the porch, but Shelby jumps when she sees us.

"Jesus, you scared me!" She has her hand wrapped around the neck of a Grey Goose, and I'm not talking about poultry. Shelby considers helping herself to the good stuff an important employee benefit of clerking at the liquor store. She drinks the vodka straight from the bottle. Tipping it my way, she asks, "You want?"

I take a few swigs, liking how chills chase up my arms. Sometimes I wonder why I bother with beer. "They like those eggs extra-pickled?"

"Huh?"

"Your eggs? The ones you're selling?"

"Oh, that." She waves a hand too expansively and bumps into Cody's drink. Luckily, he's almost through, so it doesn't spill. "I just made that up."

Figures.

"I mean, I was thinking about it. And with everyone"— here she stops and sends the Stare of Death at my mom, who is on the other side of pig-pit, laughing it up with Cody's dad—"pregnant, I thought why not? It's not like I'm ever getting married again."

Shelby is a prime example of why Rule #4, Don't Need Him, is vitally important. She thought Rob, her ex-husband was The One. She thought the Guitar Player was Mr. Forever. As soon as she starts relying on them, thinking they'll get jobs and take over her car payments, they up and leave her.

"Get a life already." I walk away. Sure, it sucks her boyfriend left her for her mom, but here again, had she followed Rule #3, Looks Aren't Everything, and fallen in love with a more average-looking guy, he would've been so grateful to be with her she wouldn't have had to worry about him ever leaving.

Cody follows me to the fire pit. Too late, I remember there is an entire pig, stick through its ass, hanging there.

"I'm going vegetarian," Cody announces.

"I'm with you." The night air is cooling, thus the reason to stand by the fire, but the smell of crispy pig flesh is too much. "Let's go inside."

In the living room, we find Dad and Shevon making out on the sofa, so we head for my room. Only Kait's in there, crying on the bed. This is not unusual in the last trimester, or so I've read. We close the door and look at each other.

"Tell me about New York, Cody." We have a shared fantasy in which we drop out of school, score fake IDs, and move to the Big Apple. A place so big that no one knows us, a place so far away our families never find us.

"There's a great place on Second Avenue and Thirteenth Street. One bedroom, affordable as long as we land jobs right away, with some famous Chinese joint below it." Cody does a lot of research on our fantasy. He looks at real-estate ads online; he knows which buses we have to catch to get there and how much our fares will cost. Periodically, he will buy a *New York Times* and circle jobs he thinks we are qualified for. Barista for me, janitorial stuff for him. It's not glamorous, but it's a dream. Our dream.

"I've got eighty bucks and some change." I slide down the stucco wall until I'm sitting on the hallway floor. The wood planks are a little gritty, but my head's buzzing and I don't care.

Cody sits Indian-style beside me. "I've got over eight hundred. We're getting there."

"Are you sure we need three thousand? Maybe we have enough to get started."

"In the city? Come on, Abs, I've shown you the cost-of-living charts."

I told you he was anal. Closing my eyes, I say, "Maybe we should shoot for somewhere cheaper. Like Montana."

Cody puts a hand behind my neck. I feel him inspecting my face. "You don't look so good."

"You sweet-talker."

"I'm serious. You're kinda pale."

I keep my eyes closed and brush away his hand. "Little woozy. Know better than to mix 'n' match."

Cody tugs me to my feet. "Come on, princess, let me put you to bed."

"Nooo." I am dead weight. I know Cody isn't strong enough to lift me on his own. That's why I'm so surprised when I feel him scoop me up, one arm under my head and one under my knees.

I flap my hands in the general direction of his chest. "Cody, put me down."

"Come on, princess," a deep voice says. A not-Cody voice. "Someone's had a little too much."

I open my eyes. Jackson has me tucked against him. I can't help my body from warming just a little. "What's with the manhandling tonight, Jack-Off?"

"Just helpin' out my little brother."

Cody is anxious, squeezing my hand, feeling my head. "You gonna hurl?"

"I'm fine," I say. Then, suddenly, I'm not.

Jackson hefts my weight and fakes like he's going to drop me. "Let's get a move on, girlie."

"Don't—" It's too late. As soon as he starts to move, my stomach heaves and vomit rockets up my throat, out and all over Jackson's shirt. It hits, splatters back on me. The smell makes me gag, and I heave again. Jackson is all, "Oh, man— gross! I can't believe you just did that."

Next, I am in the bathroom with only a fuzzy memory of Jackson and Cody maneuvering me into the shower. Cody turns the knob, and water blasts down on my fully clad body. Jackson is behind me, propping me up, sloshing barf off both of us with his hands.

"This is not how I imagined our first shower together," he whispers against my neck.

I make a halfhearted jab to his gut. "Shut up," I say. The water is clearing my head. I step out of the tub and Cody hands me a towel. I dab at my arms, my wet clothes, then give up and wrap the towel around my head.

"You're welcome!" Jackson's loud voice follows me back to my bedroom. He'd fit right in with my family.

I slam the door. Kait looks up. Her face is wet from crying. In the dim light, I can see the giant hump of her belly, moving up and down with her breath.

Flinging sopping clothes and the towel in the direction of the closet, I say, "Don't ask."

"I wouldn't."

I slip into an old T-shirt, one I've cut the sleeves off of, and huddle under my covers. Sleeping with wet hair will give me total bedhead, but I'll deal with that—and the mess in the bathroom—tomorrow.

For tonight, I watch the rise and fall of my sister's belly by the light of the overambitious streetlight in front of our house. I think about that baby and what a sucky world she's coming into. I make a silent vow to her, using my auntie-telepathic skills, that I will teach her all she needs to know to stay safe. By the time she hits puberty, I'll have her reciting my One True Love Rules like a kindergartner rattles off her ABCs.

Before I drift off, the last thing I think of is Jackson. Jackson's hands on me, his breath in my ear. His big, stupid grin. Tomorrow, I'll forget all about him. But tonight, I remember.

"I have amnesia."

Cody doesn't look surprised. Like me, he is also a fan of daytime TV. He calmly dips his toast into his coffee and bites off a soggy mouthful.

"Seriously." I etch circles in his mom's blue-checked tablecloth with my fingernail. "I woke up this morning and couldn't remember a thing about yesterday. Not. A. Thing." That much was true. But later, when I finished brushing my teeth and spit, it all came rushing back. Jackson, vomit, the shower. Amnesia seemed the best course of action.

On soap operas, there are different kinds of amnesia. There's the kind after a minor accident that only lasts a few weeks, or the kind that lasts for months and is miraculously cured during ratings-sweeps week. Then, there's the kind that happens when an actress leaves the show, but rather than kill off the character, they make her disappear for a few months and then bring her back, but played by another actress. Since the character's experience was so harrowing that even her height and facial structure is changed, she never gets her memories back. That is the kind of amnesia I have.

"You're wearing the red tank, like I told you to. Yesterday. On the phone." Cody is too observant.

"I like red. It's a coincidence."

"You don't remember the pig roast? Or Jackson coming home?" He offers me a bite of mushy toast. I don't know why he bothers to put the bread in the toaster.

My hands fly to my face. "Jackson's back? Oh my gosh!" My acting is every bit as good as you'll find on a soap.

Cody laughs and gets up to rinse off his dishes. "You ready to shop?"

"Yeah, but I gotta warn you, it's gonna be a tight squeeze in the Benz. *Everyone's* coming. The good news is the Guitar Player is driving."

Stuffing people into Mom's Mercedes like frat boys on a beer run is a family tradition. Cody has been sandwiched, squashed, and sat on for many a ride. "The only Savage butt I'm touching is yours. Got it?"

We hear Jackson's footsteps on the stairs before we see him. He props himself against the arch leading into the kitchen. "Savage Butts? Great band name. You should tell Steve."

My face burns. I stare at the white-tile floor. Then I remember that I don't remember, so I jump out of my chair with a huge smile on my face. "Jackson! When did you get back?"

I rush and give him a quick, I'm-just-the-girl-next-door hug.

Jackson looks at his brother.

"She doesn't remember," Cody says. I love him for keeping a straight face.

"Oh." Jackson rubs his head. He is sleepy-looking in a

rumpled shirt and baggy sweats. "You guys goin' somewhere?"

"No," I say, because I don't want him to tag along.

"The mall," Cody says.

Jackson pulls up a chair at the table and props his elbows on the table. "Cool, I need to pick up a few things."

"There's no room," I blurt, and it's even the truth. "And don't you have your own car anyway?"

Jackson scratches his armpit. Why I'm fascinated, I don't know. "Yeah, but I hate shopping alone. Cody, can I give you a list? Backpacking is rough on the wardrobe. Mom said I could use her credit card if I needed anything."

Unlimited access to the credit card? Cody lights up. "No problem. Tell me what you need."

I don't want to hear about underwear sizes, so I make my escape. "Come over when you're ready," I say to Cody.

He is already scribbling notes on a pad of paper, Jackson next to him at the table. It's like I'm not even there. Then Jackson catches me watching him and smiles, and I'm more alive than I've been in months. Two months, to be exact. This is not good. I recite the Rules in my head all the way back to my house.

Chapter ♥ 4

One of the few advantages of living in the middle of nowhere is that you're never far from an outlet mall. We take the I-17 south out of Cottonwood, passing miles and miles of— no surprise here—cottonwood trees, and stop at the nearest shopping center.

The Guitar Player brings us to a lurching stop in the parking lot and turns off the Meat Loaf CD that he's been blasting since we left home. My head, for about the tenth time, bangs into the metal that is exposed by the giant rip in the roof upholstery.

"Ow," Cody says for me. I've given up on complaining. Whining only makes my hangover headache worse. I take another gulp out of my water bottle and hope the rehydration kicks in soon.

"Everybody out," the Guitar Player proclaims, like we're all so comfy that we need any prompting.

Kait wriggles out of the backseat with Shelby, who first has to eject Hannah off her lap before she can struggle out of the car. Once they're gone, I roll off Cody and he lets out a sigh of relief.

"I gotta say, Abs, you're not as light as you used to be."

"Hey!" I rub my head. "Tell you what, on the way back, you sit on my lap!"

He laughs, gets out, and holds the door for me. I look back and see the Guitar Player and Mom are still in the front seat. Her arms are whipping around like they are debating something intensely. How much hair product he's allowed to buy? The danger of too much Obsession for Men to the fetus? I decide I don't care and rush to catch up to my sisters.

The first place we go is the bathroom. Because Kait is pregnant and has to pee every three minutes and because Shelby has to make sure her hair is perfect. I almost go in with them because there is always the danger that Hannah, who thinks toilets are toys, will flush whatever she can cram in the bowl. Like giant wads of toilet paper or her shoes. But, I remind myself, I'm officially off Hannah duty when Shelby's around. I'm not anybody's mother, and that's how it's going to stay.

Cody and I wait outside, watching the parade of early-morning shoppers. A major bonus of coming to this outlet mall is that some developer somewhere realized that Arizona is hotter than the surface of the sun and so wisely enclosed and air-conditioned this place. Bless that developer, wherever he may be.

One of those senior walking clubs passes by, gray-haired women and balding men in pastel soccer shorts and athletic shoes moving along at quite a clip. There's even a guy in a wheelchair who apparently gets a great upper-body workout rolling himself along the faux-marble floors.

"Will that be us someday?" I ask Cody. "Coming to the mall

for our daily exercise because we can't afford to join a gym?"

"At least we'll always know where the good sales are." His eyes scan the storefronts, ever on the alert for a red sign promising 50 percent off. "Tell me again why we're waiting for *them*?"

I shrug one shoulder a little self-consciously. "Kait wants me to help her with something."

"Oh God, we're not going shopping for maternity underwear, are we?" he groans.

"No, no," I'm quick to reassure him. "Just a few little things. Like a breast pump."

He actually looks scared until he realizes I'm joking. "You're so unfunny, you're like the anti-fun."

Hannah's the first one out of the bathroom, looking suspiciously wet. Shelby and Kait exit next, already bickering about what store to go to first.

"There's one place Kait and I are going together," I say, stepping between them, "and we're doing that now. Why don't we meet up later at the food court and you can continue your fight then?"

"Is *he* going with you?" Shelby cuts a look at Cody.

Cody lifts one shoulder. "I guess."

"Then I'm coming, too." Shelby takes Hannah's hand and pulls her along, even though I haven't said where we're going. Typical Shelby. Can't be left out of anything. Luckily, she's walking in the right direction.

It's touch-and-go as we pass the Bath & Body Works outlet, but I finally get our whole entourage on the move.

"Here we are." I stop our little parade in front of the Waldenbooks.

"What, have you got a school project or something?" Shelby asks. "Can't you just go to the library when we get home?"

"Actually, this is my stop," says Kait. She pushes hair behind her ear but doesn't go in.

Have none of them ever been in a bookstore before? Sheesh. I grab Hannah by the hand and lead her to the children's section in the back. I find a *Pat the Bunny*, my personal all-time favorite, and set her on the brown carpet. "Cody, will you keep an eye on Hannah?"

"Sure. Maybe we'll even have time for some *Green Eggs and Ham*." He crouches down beside Hannah and shows her how to pat the bunny. "Gently," he has to repeat several times before she stops trying to yank the fur out of the book.

When I get back to the front of the store, Kait and Shelby have advanced in as far as the magazines. "Come on," I say to Kait. "What was that book you wanted to find?"

She whispers like we're in a library. "Something about babies? You know, about getting ready?"

"Aren't you a little far along for that kind of crap?" Shelby follows us as I pull Kait through the rows, looking for health care or self-help or something. Hey, it's not like I'm the expert here.

Kait bites her lip, and it occurs to me maybe the whispering was because she didn't want Shelby to hear. But if you want to keep a secret in this family, you should just keep your mouth shut. Like me. My secrets are hidden in my journal under my bed—a completely safe location since no one cleans under anything at our house.

"Like this?" We are in the medical section, and there's this thick green reference book on pregnancy and birth.

Kait pulls it partially off the shelf and checks out the cover. "Maybe? I'm not sure."

"Here you go." Shelby's facing the opposite shelf, filled with self-help books. "*A Single Mom's Survival Guide.* God knows you're going to need all the advice you can get."

Kait's brown eyes get watery and she wipes at her nose. "No," she says. "That's not it, either." But she takes the book from Shelby and puts it on top of her medical tome. Then she has to dig around in her purse for a tissue. I kind of like it better when she's mad.

"Can I help you?" says a semi-cute salesguy just as Kait lets out a horn-blast of nose-blowing. She starts crying in earnest.

"Jeez, Shel, now look what you've done." I take the books from Kait and hold them for her.

Shelby holds up her hands in self-defense. "I'm just telling it like it is."

"My sister—" I start to say, but then Kait sobs and I have to wait to be heard. "Actually, we're looking for books about babies. For new moms. Like advice and stuff, I think. Right, Kait?"

Kait swallows. "I want to be a good mom. Maybe a book would help me know what to do."

"You don't need a book," Shelby scoffs. "They pop out and ruin your life all on their own."

"Shelby!" I jab a finger at her. "Remember you're not supposed to talk like that where Hannah can hear you."

"I'm not. It's not like she understands what I'm saying anyway."

"Hannah's just a couple aisles away. And you don't know what she does and doesn't understand." Although she probably understands her mom better than Shelby thinks. Which is why Hannah never puts up a fuss when she's left with babysitters.

The poor bookstore guy clearly has no idea what to say. He stands there, face getting redder and redder, until I finally say, "So, is there a maternity section or something?"

"Right over here." He takes a deep breath, clearly relieved. "There's *What to Expect When You're Expecting*, of course. *Baby's First Year*. Is that what you're looking for?"

Kait nods gratefully. Shelby snorts but stays with us. After flipping through a few books, Kait starts piling 'em up. Pregnancy, name choosing, parenting, nutrition, even an astrology guide. Finally, she scans the shelf one more time, looks over the books she's chosen, puts all but two of them back, and says, "I'm ready to go."

Cody meets us at the checkout counter, bag already in hand.

"You bought her something?" I ask. "You didn't have to do that."

"Uh, actually I did. Pat had kind of a bad-hair day." He pulls out *Pat the Bunny*. The fuzzy parts are gone. He reaches in the bag again and pulls them out.

Shelby grabs Hannah by the arm and yanks her out of the store. "You bad, bad girl!"

Cody sweeps up Hannah from behind, dislodging Shelby's grip. "She didn't know what she was doing. She's only three."

"She has to learn." Shelby holds out her arms and narrows her deadly blue eyes at Cody. "You coddling her doesn't help."

I'm right behind them, ready to scoop up Hannah if Cody and Shelby throw down. Instead, Cody says, "I'll hand her over if you promise not to punish her. It was my fault. I wasn't watching her closely enough."

Shelby snorts. "Yeah, I noticed how much help you are."

Cody's teeth grind, but all he squeezes out is, "Promise."

"Fine, I promise." She flips her hair over her shoulder. "I shouldn't have left Hannah with you anyway. You've always been completely *useless*." The stress and volume she puts on the last word makes me flinch. Other shoppers eye us carefully.

Very calmly and slowly, Cody places a clearly upset, lip-quivering Hannah feetfirst on the tile floor. Then he spins on his heel and sprints toward the nearest exit.

"Don't bother," Shelby says when she sees I'm about to take off after him. She takes Hannah by the hand and pulls her close. "You'll never get a real boyfriend carrying that kind of weight around."

"Just shut up, Shelby." I push past her, wishing I could say other, more hurtful things. But Hannah's here and for better or worse, Shelby's her mom. "We'll meet you at the food court in two hours."

Kait comes out of the store with her bag of books. She looks from Hannah to Shelby to me and says, "What happened?"

Shelby handles the explanations, because I'm out of there.

I find Cody outside the Gap outlet, staring at his own reflection in the oversized window. Other shoppers are like ghosts behind him. Even me. I approach cautiously. He sees me in the window. Doesn't turn.

"I hate your sisters." His voice is whisper soft, but I hear him loud and clear.

For some weird reason, I feel defensive of Kait. She's really trying, buying those books and thinking about the baby before she's even born. But there's no excuse for Shelby.

"Thanks for sticking up for Hannah." I stand beside him, cross my arms over my stomach. "You're the reason I didn't turn out like them. If Hannah has any kind of chance at being normal, she's gonna need you, too."

He pinches the bridge of his nose and squeezes his eyes shut. "I don't know."

I inch closer to him until our arms are touching. "Well, I know. And the truth is you're the best. And Shelby's a bitch."

He finally smiles. "Yeah, you're totally right."

Linking my arm through his, I drag him into the store. "Come on, let's do some damage on that credit card."

"Wa-*ay* too girly," Cody says from behind me. "Jackson'll never wear it."

I sling the pink polo I'm holding against his chest. "For me, dork."

He takes it from me, holds it up to my face. "Maybe, but I have a better idea."

Before I know it, I'm in the dressing room with a pile of clothes. None of which I can afford and only a few of which I picked out myself. Cody assures me his mom won't notice another fifty bucks on the card as long as we buy some stuff for Jackson here, too. Against my better judgment, I let Cody buy me a little spaghetti-strap sundress, all yellows and blues, with peek-a-boo sandals and a canvas bag. At the counter, he finds a pair of metallic flip-flops in the same shade of blue as the dress in the bargain bin and adds them to our pile.

"The dress is way hotter on you than those shorts from the sales rack. And you should definitely stay away from crew-necks, Abby. How many times do I have to tell you? Scoop or V, scoop or V."

I let him lecture me because he's paying, but I'm not really worried about necklines. The truth is, I've got more important things on my mind. Like how the sundress is the perfect outfit for launching the One True Love Plan and that now I'll be able to save some of my back-to-school clothing money for the New York Fund. Thank you, Barbara Jennings and your generous Visa card. Thank you very much.

Cody and I search the food court for my family. We find Kait sitting by herself at a table for four. The remains of a Big Mac meal litter the tray in front of her. I dodge some mall traffic and cut to her table. Cody follows.

"Where's everybody?"

Kait folds a napkin in half and dabs at the special-sauce splotch on her protruding belly. "I don't know. Shelby took Hannah to Supercuts. I was hungry. She said she'd meet us here."

"And here we are." Shelby slides into the seat across from Kait. Hannah runs up and grabs my leg.

Staring down at her, I'm struck by how much she looks like Shelby and Mom. The bowl cut is trimmed, and now her light-blue eyes dominate her rosy face. "Abby!" she sings, "Abby, Abby!"

"Hey there, Hannah-doll." I hug her with one arm. "Nice haircut."

"Mom, too!" she squeaks at me.

"Just a trim," Shelby says, fingering the ends. "Terence was working today."

"Shelby!" Kait and I say together. Terence is psycho-ex #2. Hair stylist and stalker, all in one. Thankfully, #1 moved to Taos a year ago, but Terence was harder to shake. He still cruises by the house a few times a month in his Windstar, but at least he's stopped calling at all hours of the night.

"What were you thinking?" I ask, hefting Hannah up to my hip.

"He didn't charge me for Hannah or my trim," Shelby answers, as if she is entitled to freebies, and riling up a semi-retired stalker is no big deal. "Shouldn't we head back to the car?"

Kait stares across the food court, and her face goes from mopey to giddy in two seconds flat. I follow her gaze and see Mom and the Guitar Player in the pretzel line.

Shelby notices, too, because she says, "Give it up, Kait. He's with her now. Believe me, the competition's over and the winner's been announced."

"You would see it as a competition," Kait complains. She rubs her belly like it's a crystal ball. "But we're going to be a family. This is his baby."

"Says you." Shelby's knowing grin stretches across her face.

Kait points a french fry at Shelby. "What's that supposed to mean?"

Shelby snags the fry and pops it in her mouth. "It means, you *say* the baby's his. We all know there's another guy who's just as likely to be the father."

Before, their bickering was just the normal Savage-family backdrop, but at this, my attention sharpens. Because I know exactly who the other guy is, and I happen to be holding a whole bag full of shorts and T-shirts for him.

"She's due in mid-September," I point out. They both look surprised that I've joined the conversation, but what I said is true. And September minus nine equals December, which is when Kait and the Guitar Player first hooked up. Not November. Not Jackson.

"Again, according to Kait." Shelby shifts in her seat, sees Cody, and looks the other way. "I guess we'll find out when the baby's actually born."

"Let's just go," Cody says as Mom and the Guitar Player walk up. She's swinging an enormous Victoria's Secret bag between them, the bright pink stripes glinting in the fluorescent lighting. The Guitar Player has one pretzel in his hand and Mom is taking bites out of it as he feeds it to her. God, give it a rest already. That bag better be filled with scented hand creams and body sprays, because the idea of her and *him* and smutty underwear is too much for me today.

Chapter 5

Only the second day of school and already it's started. Cody and I are walking from our lockers to home-room on Tuesday when someone rams us from behind and slams Cody against a trash can.

"Watch it!" I yell, even though I can't see who it was.

Cody wipes trash juice from the side of the can off his new boot-cut jeans. His face shows more than distaste for the gross. He is afraid.

I hand him a tissue out of my backpack. I'm pretty sure it's clean. "Don't worry. It was just an accident."

He nods but doesn't look at me. The tissue turns a splotchy brown, and he throws it away. "It's not the only thing."

"What else? Why didn't you tell me?" I promised Cody this would stop, but really, I'd just hoped it would all go away.

"Didn't want you to worry." He reaches into his back-pack and pulls out a drawstring bag. "It was in my locker this morning."

I peek inside. "What's Mr. Manly doing at school?"

My sisters gave me a dildo for my fourteenth birthday. I still haven't figured out if it was a joke, a girl-power thing, or just a statement on the sad state of teen sex in the new millennium. Whatever it was, Mr. Manly is still in his gift bag, hidden under my bed.

Cody shakes his head like he can't believe he wants to laugh. "It's not Mr. Manly." He urges me to lean in. "Look closer."

This dildo is definitely not Mr. Manly. This is Mr. Manly's older, bigger, black brother. "Oh my God. Why would they give this to you?"

He digs in his backpack. "It came with a card."

Maybe this will keep you at home.

I give Cody a hug. "It's just some jerk. Ignore them."

Cody's body quivers. "I can't do it again—not this year, not anymore. Abs, I've got to get out of this place."

"We'll tell someone. A teacher, or the principal. They'll make it stop."

On soap operas, teens are only taunted for being un-cool, which usually a makeover from a do-gooder character can cure. With Cody, it's not that simple and I understand why he's so afraid to come out. If this is how they treat him when they're not sure, how much worse will it be when they know?

"No one can help me. I don't even know who it is."

I have a hunch. When you've known someone your whole life, you pretty much know what they are capable of. Sean Evans and Craig Phelps are my two main suspects. They tortured the fetal pig in Bio last year, making it dance with its dissected insides hanging out. To Cody, I say, "We won't know unless we try."

"No." He stands up straight, takes the drawstring bag, and stuffs it into his backpack. "It's bad enough what *they* think. I won't have my teachers looking at me weird, thinking I'm . . . you know."

But you are. I don't say it, because just the word *gay* makes him wince. There are only three openly gay students at Union High, and they're mostly left alone. I don't know why Cody is singled out. Last year, he dealt with graffiti on his locker, and stupid shit like having his underwear stolen during PE and then returned the next day with a hole cut in the butt. The brush-bys in the hallways, the whispered hate. It escalated in the spring, but no matter how much I begged, he wouldn't tell anyone but me.

The bell rings. We're late. And because Cody swears me to silence, I lie to my Biology II teacher, Mr. Kimball, about having female problems. He lets it go, and I wonder what excuse Cody is giving his teacher.

Mr. Kimball asks us to get our textbooks and open to chapter four. There is a full-color blowup of a fruit fly on the first page. Ugly little buggers.

"Perhaps those of you who took Bio I with me last year remember the famous scientist Gregor Mendel and his ground-breaking experiments with pea plants?" Mr. Kimball asks in what is clearly a rhetorical tone, because he plows ahead without even looking to see if anyone is raising their hand. "Or perhaps not. There has, after all, been a summer recess, which

I suspect has had an adverse effect on your memory."

He pauses to allow time for us to laugh, then shushes us with one of his trademark looks. "Since genetics is a special interest of mine, I thought we'd jump ahead in the text and start this year off with an in-depth study of Mr. Mendel's Laws of Inheritance and how they shaped genetic research. From there, we'll finish off the unit by bringing it all to the present with a look at what's happening in genetics today."

"Like cloning?" someone in the back asks.

Mr. Kimball dances his eyebrows. "And so much more!"

"Will all this be on the AP test in the spring?" Lucas Fielding, who was in Bio I with me last year, asks. He has a new haircut—shorter around the ears and a little messy on top—that's way more flattering than the flattop he had last year.

Mr. Kimball's lips thin. He's that weird age men get when they're old, but you can't really tell their age. Forty? Fifty? He clears his throat and says in his always scratchy voice, "Never fear, Mr. Fielding, you'll be amply prepared for the Advanced Placement exam."

Lucas's shoulders relax and he flips to page seventy in the book. I use the eraser on my pencil to turn a few pages. Charts and more charts. It's going to be a long semester.

"Two more weeks." Cody kicks rocks out of his way as we walk the mile from our bus stop to home. Two more weeks until he's driving and dust up our noses as we trudge along in the August heat with overweight book bags is a thing of the past. My Bio II book alone weighs about twenty pounds. I should've left it in my locker, but something tells me I'm going to need a lot of boning up on my genetics tables if I'm going to pass this class.

A car slows down behind us. Cody tenses.

"Get in." It's Jackson in his '98 gray Corolla. "Too hot to walk in this."

I worry for a second that he'll peel out as soon as we open the doors, a trick he thought was oh so funny when he first got his license, but he doesn't. We climb into the back of the car, which Jackson has turned into an arctic zone. The A/C is so loud I can barely hear the radio.

"Rough day?" Jackson asks when neither of us speaks. He studies us in the rearview mirror. "What's that?"

Cody slaps a hand low on his neck, just under his collar. "What's what?"

"That."

"Nothing." Cody doesn't move his hand.

Jackson smiles knowingly into the mirror. "It's a hickey, isn't it? C'mon, man, 'fess up."

My eyes burn holes in the side of Cody's head. He doesn't turn. I am forced to wrestle his hand away from his neck.

"It *is* a hickey! Cody, who?"

He shrugs and turns red, and the smattering of freckles across his nose blend away. "No one you know."

"Impossible. Need I remind you how small our school is?"

Cody lowers his hand. "She's a freshman. Just forget it."

She?

"She who?" Jackson is the one who says it. Our eyes meet in the mirror.

Cody's jaw slams shut. "Nobody, okay? Leave it."

I bounce a little on the seat. "At least tell me *when*? It's the second day of school. You're not ditching already, are you? Without me?"

"Art," is all he'll say. I *knew* I should've taken that class. Everyone knows how free Ms. Sheila is with that hall pass.

We pull into their driveway, and Cody jumps out before the car is fully stopped.

Jackson turns around. "That was weird."

In a lot of ways. "He's always been private. He'll tell us when he's ready."

At least, that's what I always thought. Now I'm not so sure. Something's different with him lately, and I don't like it. I also don't like that Cody won't tell on those jerks from earlier today.

"You okay?" He must see the worry on my face. I try to fake it, but he knows me pretty well. "Tell me. Maybe I can help."

"It's nothing you'd understand." I wish Cody hadn't made me promise not to tell. I wish I didn't take that promise so seriously.

"Try me."

If Jackson was still at our school, it might be his friends teasing Cody. It wasn't that Jackson was mean to us last year, but his and my ideas of funny are pretty far apart. Like I'm supposed to find having my locker filled with a week's worth of Jackson's football-practice socks amusing. And his friends were worse, always with the bodily-fluid jokes and bra snapping. "Maybe you can guess?"

"Some guy is harassing you." His hands clench the wheel and his shoulders are rigid.

"No, not me. Guess again."

Jackson's eyes light with understanding. "Cody? What're they doing?"

I hook my pinky and wiggle it at him. "Guess."

"You promised not to tell?"

"Bingo."

He faces forward again. His shoulders slump. "Is it bad?"

"He's taking it bad."

"Yeah?"

"Yeah."

Picking my backpack up off the floor, I slide across the backseat and out the door. Jackson stops me with a honk.

I circle around to the driver's side. "What?"

"I'll drive you guys to and from school."

A mixed blessing. "Why?"

"I want to get to the bottom of this. I want to be there if he needs me."

There are a lot of reasons why riding to and from school with Jackson is not a good idea. I try to find one that he can't argue with. "Don't you have to go to A.U. soon? When does your semester start?"

"Yesterday."

"What?" My eyebrows shoot up. "Are you kidding me?"

He closes his eyes for a second. "It's no big deal. Just freshman orientation stuff. Real classes don't start until next week."

"But aren't you a freshman?"

"I'll catch up. Right now, I have some stuff I need to figure out. I can't go off to college until my head's back on straight."

I look at Jackson, really look at him. He has been Cody's

pain-in-the-ass brother for as long as I can remember. Then, oh so briefly last spring, he was my hottie next door with the melty kisses. But what I see in his eyes now has never been there before.

"You're different," I say.

"The stuff I saw on my trip to Nicaragua . . . kids, little kids, living in the streets, starving, sick, dying, and no one doing anything to help them. I don't think anyone could be the same after that. So I'm here, for a little while anyway, until I figure things out."

I search his face, his eyes, for some clue about this change in him. "Maybe someday you'll tell me more about your trip."

"Maybe."

We leave it at that.

Although Kait is a second-time senior, she isn't going to Union. She's in some kind of alternative, study-at-your-own-pace program. It's pretty sweet, because she doesn't have to attend classes. She checks in with her adviser twice a week, and in between, she studies at home. Or at least, she's supposed to study. What she's actually doing is working extra hours at the Blockbuster.

"Pleeeeeease," she begs me now from where she is propped against a mound of pillows on her bed. "I know you read it this summer. One measly paragraph, that's all I'm asking."

She is talking about me writing her summary for *The Bell Jar* by Sylvia Plath. I am disinclined to do her homework, especially considering I have plenty of my own to do. I beat a pencil against the notebook in which I'm trying to make notes about the genetic research on fruit flies. It's not going well. I'd like to blame the fact that my bed is too hard, or that the overhead light is too bright, or that Meg and Drew are distracting me with their happy-in-love smiles on poster after poster, but I fear it's just that fruit flies who got it on half a century ago are not intrinsically interesting.

"Please, please, please? I'm supposed to be at work at eight tonight. I have to leave in half an hour, and I haven't even showered yet. I'll never get this stupid essay done by tomorrow." Kait's voice cracks like she's about to start crying.

When I think about how much she has cried lately, I decide to do my future niece a favor and keep her mother away from Sylvia's depressed and suicidal work.

"Sure, I'll do it," I say, deciding that perhaps the *Kate and Leopold* poster is hurting my concentration. Hugh Jackman is beaucoup distracting.

"You will?" Kait's mouth actually drops open like you see in cartoons, but her tongue doesn't roll across the ground.

I push my own homework onto the floor. "Are there guidelines or anything?"

I'll tell you my secret. The main reason I do well in school is that I read the directions for every assignment and do exactly what the teacher asks for. No more, no less.

Kait hands me a paper that is—surprise, surprise—tear-stained. "Thanks, Abs. I didn't think you would."

I'm not sure what to say to that. As I read the assignment, I see that it is not *one measly paragraph* but in fact an opinion essay with a minimum of five paragraphs. My future niece better appreciate the sacrifices I'm making for her.

"Abby?" Kait worries a fingernail between her teeth. She won't bite it off, just sort of sucks it until the nail polish peels. "Can I ask you something?"

"I'm not doing your math, too." I twirl my pencil while thinking of a stunning opening line for her essay. I look to Hugh for inspiration but he's no help.

"Do you think Steve still loves me?"

"What?" I drop the pencil. "The Guitar Player? *That* Steve?"

Nail-polish chips gather on the shelf of her belly. "Of course that Steve. At the pig roast, he said some stuff."

The jerk. "What stuff?"

"How when the baby came, he hoped we could all be a family. A real family like on TV." She reaches under her pillow and brings out one of the books she bought at the mall. She taps the cover of *Dr. Patty's Guide to Peaceful Parenting*. "Dr. Patty says a child creates an immutable bond between a man and a woman that lasts for life. Don't you think that's what Steve means? That we're tied together forever and we have to do our best to make a happy home for our kid?"

I try to think of a happy family on one of my soaps. Drawing a blank. "Are you sure he was talking about *your* baby?"

Kait glares at me. "What else?"

"Um, Mom's baby?"

She starts to say something back, but gasps and grabs her belly instead. Her face contorts and I think she's going to cry again.

"Hey, I didn't mean—" There is liquid dripping down Kait's leg. "Kait, what's happening?"

She pants. "Too early, this is too early. . . ." She cries out and tries to stand. Her legs collapse, and now she is lying on our hardwood floor, tears pooling beside her head, something else pooling under her legs.

I shove aside the sheets hanging on our window and check the driveway. No Mercedes. Kait's car is there, but I don't know how to drive a stick yet. She was supposed to teach me but always managed to blow off our plans at the last minute.

"Ooh," she moans, and squeezes her thighs together. "She's not due until *September*—how can this be happening now?"

Oh crap, oh crap, oh crap.

"Abby, help me." Her eyes are glazed with pain.

I pick up the phone. Mom's in Phoenix with the Guitar Player at a show, and Shelby's at work. I call Cody, even though I'm not exactly sure what he can do. Only it's not Cody who answers on the first ring.

"Jackson, I—" I can't get the words out. "It's Kait, she's—I think she's . . . oh God . . ."

"Hang on, Abby. I'll be there in three seconds." Jackson hangs up.

"He's coming." I see my sister on the floor, both hands gripping her stomach, legs shaking. "Can I help get you on the bed?"

"N-no." Her teeth chatter. Her body is still, knees curled against the bottom of her big belly.

There are a lot of surprise labors on *Veterans' Hospital*, so I know that I should rush off and get towels or boil water, but I don't want to leave my sister. I whip the comforter off Kait's bed and tuck it around her. Then I do the only other thing I can think of. I get down on the floor, pillow her head in my lap, take her hand in mine, and hang on.

Chapter ♥ 6

We are born in pain.

It is a great first line for Kait's *Bell Jar* essay. Too bad there is nothing to write on in the waiting room. Cody and Jackson are camped out in the stiff plastic chairs closest to the muted TV. They are the only ones here with me.

On *Moments of Our Lives,* when someone is in the hospital, all the characters gather and pace the corridors, drink coffee, and rehash all the plot threads. Emotions run high. There is arguing and beaucoup drama. My family won't even come to the hospital.

"I can't leave work," Shelby said when I called her on Cody's cell phone. "You know evenings are my busiest time at the store." Apparently, most people like to buy their booze after five p.m. Before hanging up, she added one more thing, which I just can't seem to get out of my head.

"Abs," she said, "going into labor today doesn't necessarily make the baby premature. Think about it." But I really don't want to dwell on August birthday versus September due date, or who the baby's dad is or isn't. I just want someone to meet me at the damn hospital!

Mom and the Guitar Player are unreachable. I left messages on their cells and on our home phone. Now, I pace the entirely too small room. FAMILY AREA, the sign on the door says. It's better than when we first arrived two hours ago and had to sit in the ER waiting room with twenty other people, most of them coughing or bleeding, trying to keep Hannah from eating an old bag of chips someone'd left behind. Thank God Barbara showed up after a quick call from Cody and took Hannah off our hands. The Family Area is private, quiet, but after another tense hour of waiting, I want to break down the door, run screaming down the halls.

"How long does it take to have a baby?"

"Relax," Cody says. "Shelby took hours, remember?"

Hannah's birth was a big deal, like everything Shelby does. Kait was her breathing coach since Hannah's dad was out of the picture long before the divorce was final, and Shelby insisted we all be in the room for Hannah's arrival. Cody was spared the sight, but I will carry that bloody, slimy memory to the grave. They really should wipe a baby off before they show it to anyone. I totally respect Kait's desire to be alone in the delivery room.

I squeeze myself into the empty chair between Cody and Jackson. Leaning my head on Cody's shoulder, I breathe deeply and slowly. He shifts and readjusts us until he gets an arm around my shoulders.

"Better?"

"I hate this."

"We're here with you," Cody says. "We're not going any-where."

I keep breathing, try to think about Kait's essay. Will her adviser believe she wrote it before the labor hit?

Jackson stretches his legs out in front of him and toes off his Nikes. "Might as well get comfortable. We could be here for hours."

It feels late. Jackson drove us here at approximately the speed of light, but I haven't seen the time since they whisked Kait to a back room just after eight thirty. No one else is in the room with us. It's like we're in a bubble, out of time and place. Only Cody's arm around me feels real, the sound of Jackson's raspy breath beside me. I feel Cody's fingers comb through my hair, which usually relaxes me but isn't working tonight.

Sitting, waiting, is driving me nuts. Cody, too. In the first five minutes, he straightened all the chairs, rearranged the fake plants according to height, and adjusted the blinds on the one window so they were level. Now he's stuck with nothing to do but pick imaginary—I hope!—flecks of dandruff out of my hair. I want to do something, anything. The first line of Kait's essay rolls through my head again. I sit up.

"Do you have a pen?" I ask. "Or any paper?"

"Nope." Cody's chin bumps my forehead when he talks.

Jackson fishes a pen out of his front pocket. "No paper, though. Sorry."

"This is great." It's a felt-tip, much better for writing on skin than a ballpoint. I click it open and start. It's good that I'm wearing a tank top. The first line goes on my upper arm.

We are all born in pain.

✳ ✳ ✳ ✳ ✳

"Not too bad." Jackson is done reading. My left arm and both legs are covered in sentences.

"It's a little rough," I say.

Jackson rubs the two-day-old shave on my legs. "No kidding."

I slap his hand away. "Hands off the masterpiece."

"That reminds me," he says. "You still writing poetry? Like the ones you showed me? They were really good."

Breath hitching, I stare at my ink-covered knee. He's not supposed to remember *that*, the *me* that was such a sap I actually wrote poems about us. And everything else, too. Friends and enemies, the environment, politics, my favorite shows. The truth is, I still do write poems. Usually late at night, in the journal I keep under my bed next to Mr. Manly. But I don't say yes to Jackson's question.

"You ever gonna return that book?" I ask. Not only had I shown him my poems, I'd lent him my favorite book, *The Essential Rumi*, a translation of writings from the thirteenth-century poet Jalal al-Din Rumi that I never cease to find completely amazing.

"Maybe I'm rereading it." He flicks hair out of his eyes. His eyes shift away.

Like I'm supposed to believe that. "If you lost it, just say so."

"I love Rumi," he protests.

I'm not impressed he remembers the name. It was in big black letters on the cover. I am about to tell him I want a new hardcover, that he won't get away with some used bookstore paperback replacement, when the door from the hallway opens.

I pop out of my seat, hoping for news. But it's Mom, thin

body wrapped in a tight black dress that shows off her long legs. Her hair is curled and flows down her back in layered waves.

"Kait's still in labor," she announces as if we don't know why we're here. She paces the room just like a *Veterans' Hospital* character would. "Three weeks early! My goodness! And can you believe that nurse wouldn't even let me in the room? Said Kait doesn't want me there. Me, her own mother!"

And rival for the affection of her baby's father. I don't say that, though. Unlike everyone else in my family, I've outgrown the need to stir things up. Slumping onto the floor, I take the pen and design a tattoo for my ankle.

"She's been in there for over three hours," Cody says after checking the time on his phone. "Did the nurse give you any more information?"

"No, no—just told me to take a seat in the maternity ward Family Area and they'd let me know. Not an easy place to find, this little room," Mom says.

I look up from my swirling vine. "Where's the Guitar Player?" The father.

Mom totters on her extra-high heels. "You know he had a gig down in Phoenix. That's where we were. I took the car. He's staying with a friend tonight, and she'll drive him up here tomorrow." She manages to look both annoyed and pathetic as she settles on the edge of one of the end tables.

Not even here for the birth of his child. Living, breathing proof that I am dead-on accurate when it comes to Rules #3 and #4, Looks Aren't Everything and Don't Need Him. You should never *need* any guy, especially one as good-looking as the Guitar Player. I'm only guessing, but my bet is the friend he's staying with is a gorgeous Guitar Groupie.

"Where are Shelby and Hannah?" Mom asks, just now noticing that it is mostly the neighbors waiting it out in the Family Area. You'd think there'd be another family crowded in here with us, waiting for their own good news, but Tuesday's apparently not a big night for deliveries in Cottonwood.

I tell her and watch as her mouth thins into a tight line. She thinks that all of us crammed into three bedrooms makes us close, but that's only geography. Her eyes take in the writing on my arm and legs. "What's this? You're not getting a tattoo, are you?"

"Yes, I'm having Kait's English essay tattooed on all visible parts of my body." I add more inky swirls to my ankle and a few angry dots.

Mom sighs like I'm the problem child in this family. "It's not flattering."

"It's not supposed to be. Got any paper in your purse?" If I don't transfer the essay soon, accidental brushes against other people or even a little sweat could destroy my work.

She tosses her purse to me. I rifle through it. Gum, crackers, wallet. "Can I use this receipt?" It's a long one from the grocery store. If I write tiny and abbreviate, it could work.

The door opens and a nurse enters. "Ms. Savage?"

"Yes?" Mom and I say together.

The nurse talks to Mom. "Your daughter wants to see you now."

I am the one who held her hand until Jackson got to the house and helped her to the car. I am the one who filled out the twelve hundred pages of medical forms. I am the one who sat for hours on the uncomfortable waiting-room chairs. I am the one dying to know how my sister is.

"Oh, thank God." Mom puts a hand to her heart and hurries after the nurse. The door closes behind her. It's the three of us again, back in our bubble. Another hour passes while we discuss what is or is not worth watching on TV this season.

"I'm gonna find a vending machine." Cody stands and stretches. "You want anything?"

I shake my head, but Jackson gives him a dollar, asks for a soda. Cody leaves. Now there are only two in the bubble.

"You don't have to do that now," Jackson says. "I mean, Kait does have a pretty good excuse for not handing it in on time."

I am scribbling out the essay on the receipt, checking my arm for details, squishing up letters tight on the page. "I know."

"You could tell me what's bothering you."

I scribble. He waits. Ignoring him, I finish transferring words from my arm and move to the first leg. It's hard to see the side of my thigh, so I twist myself around.

Jackson kicks back in his chair, turning sideways so he can throw his legs over the side. "Or not. I could tell you what's bothering me."

I raise my head and our eyes lock. I don't want to know, but I do.

"There was this girl," he starts. Disgusted, I turn away. He goes on. "This girl, she lived next door and I was crazy about her."

I am slightly more interested. I live next door to him, but

then I remind myself he could easily be talking about one of my sisters. Or, God forbid, my mom.

"But my brother was in love with her. I tried to stay away, but I couldn't. I was always hanging out at her place, doing stupid stuff to make her laugh."

True. He used to be at my house as much as Cody. And he did act stupid, bragging about his football season or how much some other girl liked him. He was pretty insufferable, actually.

"So this girl, she had an older sister. Not as hot as she was, but my age. We ended up at the same party right before Thanksgiving break where we both had a few too many Wild Turkey shots. She was cute, friendly, flirty—a little of this led to a little of that. I thought maybe it could work, but after we saw each other a few more times, she acted weird. All mysterious. Said what happened between us didn't mean anything because she was in love with someone else. You know who that was?"

I nod. Kait and the Guitar Player, who else?

"But then that jerk dumps her and goes for her older sister. Next, he moves on to her mom. It's pretty outrageous, but the upside is that the girl, the first one that I liked so much—suddenly she's always at my house. Watching TV with my brother, staying for dinner. Even spending the night. She's everywhere I go—home, school—and the more I get to know her, the crazier I am about her."

I have to admit that I'm liking this story more and more. Smiling, I wait for him to continue.

"And then I start to panic because months have gone by. Sometimes I think I don't have a shot. Sometimes I think what a rotten thing it would be to steal her away from my own brother. But even though I try, I can't stop thinking about her.

"So I talk to my brother and I say dude, if you love this girl, go for it. What're you waiting for? And get this, he says, 'She's my best friend. I don't love her like that.' I'm like, whoa, maybe I do have a chance. But I better move fast because graduation's less than a month away and then I'm going to Nicaragua for the summer."

As he talks, I'm drawn closer to him. I'm sitting on the floor. My leg brushes his chair.

Jackson swings forward so his knees are outside of mine and he's staring down at me. "Do you remember that night? When I talked you into studying for our finals together?"

I swallow. I remember, too well, his lips against mine, his hand in my hair. Our first kiss. We never did make flash cards.

"A week. That's what's bothering me, Abby. A week wasn't enough for us."

I want to agree with him. I want to lunge into his arms and let him hold me until my sister is okay. Kiss me until I forget we're in the hospital. But that is what a soap-opera hero-ine would do. She would let the passion of the moment sweep away her judgment, plunge her back into a relationship that can never work. It's a good thing that I have my Plan. The Rules will save me.

"Jackson," I stall. "Shelby says you're the father of this baby. Is it possible?"

His big hand reaches down and cups my chin. "Did we have sex? Yes. But I'm not this baby's dad."

It's almost enough, that certainty in his voice. His face leans closer to me. We are inches apart, and I can feel the warm exhale of his breath against my lips. But the idea that for even one second I might end up with my niece's father makes me feel like I've sucked down one too many sourballs.

"Jackson," my voice comes out as scratchy as the carpet I'm sitting on, "I'm sorry. I can't do this."

Our eyes meet. He is about to say something else, something that will maybe change my mind because it is hard to fight my *want* when he is so close.

But Cody opens the door and says, "Guess what?"

I jump to my feet. "Is it over? They're okay?"

"They're both fine. It's a girl, five pounds and eleven ounces. We're all invited to meet her right now."

"The vending machine told you?" I ask, glancing pointedly at the two sodas in his hand.

"I ran into your mom on the way back. Do you want to give me a hard time or are you coming already?" Cody takes my hand, and we run down the hallway.

We stand outside the baby room, at the big picture window, and look at my niece in one of the tiny beds. She is red and wrinkly, but at least they've cleaned her off so I have a better first impression of her than I did of Hannah. She is perfectly beautiful, and I already love her so much my heart hurts.

Then I see the name card. "She didn't."

"What?" Jackson comes up behind us. He puts a hand on my shoulder. I fight not to lean into him.

"Look at the name."

"Stephanie? That's a nice name," Cody says.

"Stephanie?" I repeat. "As in the feminine of Stephen, as in Steve the Guitar Player, who is both this child's father and stepgrandfather?"

Cody laughs. "Oh my gosh, Abs, your family is better than any show on TV."

"Shut up." I punch him in the arm. "We are not."

Cody hums the tune to "I'm My Own Grandpa." And I have to admit it. He's right. My family belongs on *Jerry Springer.*

Chapter 7

Wednesday morning, and even though my sister has just given birth, Mom decides it's better for me to go to school than hang out at the hospital all day. I shuffle into Bio II, decked out in my new sundress, only to find a note instructing us to go to the lab instead. That Mr. Kimball, always trying to keep us on our toes.

"Welcome to Bio Lab!" Mr. Kimball chants as we file in and take seats on the stools at each station. Because Cody's not in this class, I don't look for anyone, don't save a spot.

Once we're all settled, Mr. Kimball pulls on his seriously chartreuse tie and says, "Today, we'll be playing an exciting game called 'Who's My Buddy?' If you win, you get an interesting, serious-minded lab partner who understands the assignments and helps you pass this class. If you lose, well, sorry folks, you'll get one of those lab partners who never does their share of the work and attempts to cheat off you during quizzes."

"Mr. Kimball?" Shauna Moore asks from her seat in the back. "Can't we choose our own partners? That's how Ms. Tatum does it in U.S. History."

"Ms. Tatum has her ways, I have mine." Mr. Kimball twists his tie, wrinkling it and showing its raspberry-colored back side. "Listen up, fellow scientists. I'll read out the lab-partner assignments, and you smile or groan accordingly. Not that it matters. There will be no trading, no switching, no complaining. Got it?"

He doesn't wait for an answer, just plows on through the list. As a Savage, I'm used to being near the end of most alphabetical arrangements, so I tune out and study my newly painted-just-for-school Purple with a Purpose nails. I'm picking at a tiny bubble on my thumbnail when Mr. Kimball calls my name.

"Yes?" I answer, forgetting that he's assigning partners and no response is necessary. There is snickering from certain people in the class. I definitely recognize Carolyn Schmitz's gurgly laugh. You'd think she'd get surgery for that or something.

"You and Mr. Fielding," Mr. Kimball is kind enough to repeat.

Lucas Fielding? He was in my Bio I class last year and asked a million questions. I guess that's not a bad quality in a lab partner.

When Mr. Kimball's done, we have to shuffle around so we're sitting with our partner. I stay on my stool, cute new metallic baby-blue flip-flops dangling in the air, and wait for Lucas to find me. He's a total brain so it doesn't take him long.

"Hey, Abby," Veronica Ortega, who is also in my computer class, says as she passes me on the way to the front row. "Guess you're a winner, huh?"

Meaning Lucas Fielding is definitely someone you want

to cheat off. She got Andy Nichols for her partner. Hot *and* smart—lucky girl.

"You, too," I say to her, and turn to my lab partner. "Hi."

"Hi." His one eye looks at me. The other one does . . . not. It appears to find my right cheek quite fascinating. I'm not sure where to look so I focus on his nose.

"I'm taking all AP classes this year, but I haven't seen you in any others," Lucas says, his nostrils flaring as he speaks.

I try meeting the eye that's looking at me. "After I took regular Bio I with Mr. Kimball last year, he asked me to move up to this class. I like science." Lame-o answer, but there it is. I've never had a teacher specifically request that I keep taking classes with them. I couldn't say no.

"Cool." He folds his hands on top of his camouflage binder.

The lab is buzzing with noise, but Lucas and I have apparently run out of things to say. Thankfully, Mr. Kimball thumps a book on the front table to get our attention.

"Now that you're all acquainted, let's go over some lab basics. The school district, in its unrelenting quest to avoid lawsuits, has declared that simply giving you a handout on safety procedures is not enough." He passes out a sheet with guidelines on it about what to do if you splash chemicals in your eyes or accidentally set something on fire. Maybe the school-district powers that be were onto something. I'd never actually read the rules before.

"Instead of my traditional fifteen-minute lecture on common sense, we'll be spending all of this period on how to not kill yourself during an experiment. After today, we'll meet here in the lab every Wednesday. Okay, if everyone would open the cabinet under your table and pull out the safety goggles . . ."

I let Lucas rummage through our cabinet as I keep reading. In case of explosion? Flying glass? Toxic gas? I never knew science class could be so exciting.

"Is Kait home? Is the baby healthy?" Gustavo, Kait's manager at Blockbuster, sounds a little frantic. When I'd met him at the store a few times, he'd always seemed pretty mellow. You wouldn't think Kait having a baby would cause major problems, especially since it's not like he couldn't see it coming.

"She's fine," I say, holding the kitchen phone between my ear and shoulder as I stir the SpaghettiOs I'm making for Hannah's dinner. "The baby, too."

"Oh, thank God," he says, and I hear him let out a long breath. This is not an employer worried over a missed shift. This is someone who cares.

I supply more info. "Kait and the baby will be home sometime tomorrow. The day in the hospital was just a formality, since she went into labor so early." *If* it was early, but I don't say that to him.

"Thank God," he says again.

Gustavo is in his mid-twenties and was one of the first employees at our local Blockbuster when it opened ten years ago. He's a little on the nerdy side, with his hair perpetually pulled back in a ponytail and glasses always slipping off his face. He's not someone new and I don't know what kind of baggage he might have, but he's not bad-looking. He doesn't fit my Rules, but it occurs to me he might be perfect for Kait.

"Come by Friday night," I say. "I'm sure Kait would love to see you."

"She would? I mean, sure, I'll stop by. What time?"

I tell him to come by after dinner and to bring a movie. It's the first time I've thought about applying my One True Love Plan to someone else. Would it work for my sisters? For Cody? I'm worried about him. What's with the hickey and the mysterious freshman girl?

"Abby!" Mom hollers from her bedroom.

"What?" I holler back, turning down the heat and setting aside the wooden spoon. I take a sip of water and watch the Os bubble.

"Abby!" she yells again, and I realize she's not going to let it go.

In her bedroom, the last one down the hall, the blinds are closed. Mom lies diagonally across the unmade bed. One arm is flung over her face. The other rests on her belly. At a little over three months pregnant, the only sign that my little sister is in there is the slightest rise that's only visible if you knew how flat Mom's stomach was before.

Despite Mom's assurances to the contrary, I'm sure the baby's a girl. I wonder if she'll look like Hannah or more like the Guitar Player. Will she have musical talent? Be a great dancer? It's too bad the only gift my dad seems to have passed on is his high tolerance for alcohol.

"Will you get me my migraine pills?" Mom whispers.

"No."

She moves her arm from over her eyes. "What did you say to me?"

"You can't take those things when you're pregnant. I don't want an eleven-toed sister." I put on my I'm-serious face. The one she should use with me, not the other way around. But I'm used to her abdicating the Momness guise in favor of her more popular role as just-one-of-the-girls.

"Abby! You can't expect me to go through a migraine without my pills. The pain!" She curls into a ball.

"I'll bring you a Tylenol."

"You know those don't work."

I suspect that Mom's migraines are actually hangovers. I've been able to add two plus two for a long time, and I don't think it's a coincidence that she often gets the headaches after the partying.

Mom moans and curls herself up tighter. I bring her a Tylenol and a glass of water and help her sit up so she can swallow.

"Will you call Steve for me? Will you tell him I need him to come home?"

Need him. It's the kiss of death for Mom's relationships, but she's hurting so I agree. He doesn't answer. I leave a message on his voice mail. I wonder if I will have to be Mom's breathing coach and if so, can I get PE credit for it?

I'm on my way to Computers on Thursday afternoon, cutting through the herd of other students rushing to beat the bell, when I see Cody up ahead. He's walking with a girl I've never seen before. I wonder if she's The Freshman.

"Cody!" I hurry to catch up.

He says something to the girl and she keeps walking.

"Is that her?"

"What? No! Are you kidding me?" He moves his backpack from one shoulder to the other.

Today, two days after the Big Hickey Incident, the mark is nearly gone. Is he planning to get a new one? "You can't hold out forever."

His eyes narrow. "There's nothing to tell. Drop it, Abby. It was a stupid mistake."

I'm trying to decide if it was a stupid mistake to make out with a *girl*, or if the stupid part was telling me it was a girl when it wasn't.

"That reminds me," he says, even though we haven't been talking, just walking toward the lockers. "There's a new guy in my speech class. Transfer student."

Speech is a requirement that you can take any year. Most people put if off until they're seniors. I took it last year to get it out of the way.

"Senior?" I ask, because so far he is Someone New and if he's a senior, it means he may well be leaving town after graduation. Two out of five is a good start.

Cody shrugs. "Yep. Swing by after last period and I'll point him out to you."

"Sounds like a plan." Cody drops me off at the computer room. How will I concentrate on the intricacies of spreadsheet management when it's possible that my One True Love Plan may actually go into effect today?

I take a seat at my computer, passing Veronica on the way with a quick wave. My computer whirs and opens up the spreadsheet I've been working on. I should tell Cody that thanks to Mr. Edwards and his insistence that we learn office tools, I may be qualified for a slightly better job in New York than simple barista. Abby Savage, administrative assistant. Has a nice ring to it.

Cody lingers outside the door of Speech. I am running late, so the hallway has mostly cleared.

"Did I miss him?"

"There." Cody points out a guy walking away from us. He's a little taller than me, not too buff, dark hair.

"Come on!" I pull him along. "If we go out the side door, we can catch him at the exit." We hurry and converge with the new guy just as he bangs out the doors of the language-arts building.

His face is average—brown eyes, regular nose, nice cheekbones, lips a little on the thin side. In other words, he's perfect. Not too good-looking, not totally hideous. He walks away, crossing the sidewalk toward the science building, completely unaware that I'm possibly his One True Love.

"His family just moved here from Phoenix." Cody fills me in as we cut across a landscaping bed filled with yarrow plants, their white flattop flowers squashed by people like us using their home as a shortcut. "No girlfriend back home."

Now this guy is three for five. Possibly four if there's not an ex, either. And as for Rule #4, Don't Need Him, that's completely up to me. Practically a perfect score and I haven't even met him yet.

"What's his name?" I ask the one thing Cody hasn't filled me in on.

"Brian. Brian Hart."

And I think what a nice, ordinary name it is. He probably has a sister named Jennifer and a little brother named Mike. They live in a two-story house with a pool, and their parents are still married. In fact, their parents never fight.

"Just one thing." Cody stops once we're back on the sidewalk and makes me spin in a circle. "Uh-huh, I thought so. Give me those." He holds out a hand.

"What?" I fidget with my earlobe self-consciously.

He tunnels fingers into my hair and emerges with the two clips I used to hold back my bangs. "What did I say about these? Only with the red tank, remember?"

"I need those!" I protest as the hair that really needs to be trimmed hits me right in the eyes.

"Red clips with that yellow T-shirt? Who do you think you are, Ronald McDonald?" He pockets my hair accessories. "You'll thank me later."

Cody jogs ahead of me. "Brian! Wait up!"

What? This isn't right. I need to prepare, get my story straight, have some kind of cute-but-not-too-cute line ready. Instead, Brian turns around with a hesitant smile on his face while Cody points at me and says something I can't hear since

I'm walking very s-l-o-w-l-y in their direction. I stop to let a small lizard scamper across the pavement in front of me.

"Hey," Brian says when I finally get to them. Up close, he is even more perfectly imperfect than I imagined. He actually has a zit on his chin.

"Hey," I say, bobbing my head. "I'm Abby. How's it going?"

"Good. How 'bout you?"

I nod. He smiles. Cody looks pleased. It is silent for an awkwardly long time. My eyes look everywhere except at Brian. The GO, COYOTES, GO! banner hanging over the door to the science building, the flag outside the main office flapping in the light breeze, Audrey Renaldo picking the underwear out of her butt as she walks by. Note to self, adjusting your panties in public is not nearly as inconspicuous as you think, no matter how quickly you do it.

"So, uh, Cody," Brian says, "what're you working on for our first Speech project?"

Cody pushes me closer to Brian. "Not sure yet. You have anything planned?"

Brian pauses a moment then looks right at Cody. "I'm thinking about doing something on gay rights. You know, marriage, adoption, that kind of thing."

Cody flushes. I can actually feel the increased body heat from where I stand. His teeth grind.

"Because most people don't really think about it, you know?" Brian continues, clearly unaware that Cody is about to blow. "But the world is changing and we have to make adjustments. Being gay is hardly the taboo issue it used to be. The laws need to change." He pauses for a breath. "Don't you think so?"

"That's not funny," Cody snarls. "You don't even know me. How dare you . . ." He trails off, shakes his head, and storms away.

Brian watches him go, and I am truly sad. Because he'd seemed to perfectly fit my rules, but as I watch him watch Cody, I see that he's not perfect for me. He's perfect for Cody.

"Don't worry." I pat Brian's arm. Now that he's no longer The One, I'm not nervous. "I'll make it right with him."

Brian's smile is shy. "I was just trying to find out if, well, maybe he's . . ."

"I know," I say. "Cody's a real catch." How to say this delicately? "He just doesn't know it yet? You know?" The look I give him is meaningful.

His face brightens. "Really? So he is gay?"

I can't tell him something Cody's never told me. "You'll have to ask him. He's never mentioned it."

"But he said you were his best friend."

"I am."

Brian nods like he finally understands.

"Be patient," I say. "He's worth it." Not to mention, it's not like Brian's got a lot of choices at Union. "In the meantime, why don't you come to my house tomorrow night and watch a movie with us?"

"Really? That's so nice."

"It's no trouble." I dig around in my bag until I find a pen and jot down my address on a scrap of paper. "Here. Around seven?"

He takes the note and folds it carefully before putting it in his shirt pocket. "It's hard to be the new guy. Thank you, Abby."

"Wait until after you meet my family. Then we'll see how thankful you are."

Chapter ♥ 8

Gustavo shows up with, like, ten movies from the Blockbuster. Kait makes a big deal out of helping him choose which one to watch. Then she makes an even bigger deal about him sitting next to her on the sofa, and quicker than you can say, "Boy, are those Savage girls fast," Kait's cuddled up next to him, Stephanie-in-the-baby-sling wrangled to the side so Kait can rest her cheek against Gustavo's arm. Poor Gustavo probably doesn't realize this is most likely a show she's hoping the Guitar Player will at least hear about if he doesn't catch the premiere tonight.

"Stephanie looks so much like her dad from this angle," Shelby says from where she sits with Hannah on her lap in the Barcalounger. She gazes at Jackson when she says, "Must be the nose."

Kait smiles, missing Shelby's meaning by a mile. "I think so, too! Amazing, isn't it, how much she looks like Steve?"

"Something's amazing." Shelby shoots a smug look Jackson's way that he completely misses. He and Cody sit on big pillows on the floor, flipping through the DVDs that Gustavo brought.

Mom's nursing another *headache* in her bedroom, waiting for the Guitar Player to keep his word and finally come home. His long weekend gig has turned into an eight-day vacation, and Mom's about had it. It's up to me to play hostess, popping corn in the kitchen.

"Abby." A hand lands on my shoulder and I jump like one of the kernels in the microwave.

"Jackson, you scared me!" I put some distance between us by going to the fridge and pulling out a couple bottles of soda. The overhead light is half burned out, making the kitchen seem too intimate.

"Sorry." He leans a hip against the Formica countertop. "Already saw this movie so I thought I'd make myself useful in here."

"What did they finally decide on?" I can hear opening credit–type music.

"Is this Brian guy your new boyfriend?" Jackson ignores my question, shoves an empty pitcher against the ice dispenser on the freezer door. He is as at home here as he is at his own house. Maybe more. Barbara likes her kitchen just so, with all the spices arranged alphabetically and the canned goods stored by size. The boys were never what you'd call welcome in her domain. "Cody said he's your new *friend*."

I want to deny it, but again, the whole situation is sensitive and I'm hoping he is a friend, although I wouldn't say it in quite that tone. "Not exactly," I say.

"Not exactly what?"

"Cody introduced us yesterday. He's new here, no other friends. You know how it is. So I invited him over. It's no big deal." At least, I hope it's no big deal. When I finally tracked down Cody after the Big Brian Blowup, he agreed that perhaps he'd overreacted and that he'd behave tonight.

I open white cupboard doors badly in need of some touch-up paint, searching for the popcorn bowls. Shelby never puts things back where they go. The water glasses are stashed over the sink instead of closest to the fridge, where I like them. And she's put the metal strainer on top of the nonstick pans, which is just a crime.

"No. Big. Deal." Jackson says after a really long silence punctuated only by me opening and slamming doors. He grabs plastic cups from the shelf and restacks them on the counter. "Cody says you have some crazy plan for getting your next boyfriend."

Cody had no right to say anything about my Plan to his brother. "Next? How about first?"

Jackson swings around and slams his fist on the butcher-block island. "*I* am your first boyfriend."

"One week hardly qualifies you as a boyfriend."

"Are you saying I don't count?" His knuckles turn white where he presses them against the wood.

I peel a stick of butter, because there's no such thing as too much butter on your popcorn, and put it in the microwave. Push 30 SECONDS. "Yeah, that's what I'm saying."

My back is to him so I don't see his face when he makes

that strange, strangled sound, but suddenly, he is behind me, his hands on my waist.

He leans down so his lips are so close to my neck I feel his breath when he speaks. "I count, Abby."

The doorbell rings and although there are fifty other people in the house who could get it, I shove my way past Jackson. "Brian's here. Relax, Jack-Off, and be nice to him."

Jackson growls something low, but I hear him take the drinks into the living room.

"Brian! Everyone's here. Come on back." I lead the way, but not before noticing Brian has spiffed himself up for the occasion.

I hope Cody notices, too.

We are halfway through *Raiders of the Lost Ark*, which Gustavo claims is a classic, when the three glasses of Diet Coke I've downed hit me.

"Back in a sec," I say, thinking no one is paying attention anyway, but when I come out of the bathroom, Jackson is waiting.

"We weren't done talking." He leans against the wall, angled so his body fills the hallway.

"I was." I attempt to dart past him.

He blocks my way. "Abby, why won't you spend five minutes alone with me? Don't I deserve that much?"

My breathing goes all weird when I'm around him, like there's only so much air in the world and he's using it all up. I start to feel light-headed. "I don't want to miss the end of the movie." Although I'm pretty sure Indiana Jones will save the girl and find the ark.

"I was stupid," he says, and that gets my attention. "I should've made you understand as soon as Shelby told you about me and Kait, but I thought you'd calm down. That I'd have the chance to convince you that what happened in November didn't have anything to do with us. Only you wouldn't talk to me, and by the time I realized how badly I'd handled everything, it was graduation. Then my trip to Nicaragua. Please don't let it be too late, Abby."

Jackson's dark-blue eyes look almost black in the poorly lit hallway. The cream walls have darkened with age, and there's a lighter square where a photo of my dad used to hang. I wonder who took it down? Probably the Guitar Player since I can't imagine it bothering anyone else. I'd taken that picture in eighth grade when Dad and I went to the Tuzigoot National Monument. It was a great day, just the two of us. He was laughing when I snapped the photo, mouth open, sun glaring off his high forehead. He thought it was an awful picture of him, but I loved it.

My finger traces the blank space on the wall as I suck in an uneven breath. I don't want Jackson to explain, I don't want to understand. I just want to move on with my Plan.

Then he leans down and kisses me. Lightly, the softest touch against my lips, and I feel myself slipping away, slipping back in time. I push against his chest, breaking the kiss, and plaster myself against the opposite wall.

"Happy birthday," I say, proud to think of something to distract him. "Wasn't it last month?"

He looks confused for a second then nods. "Yeah."

"You know what that makes me?"

We stare at each other. He takes a step toward me.

"Jailbait."

He stops dead. "You're almost sixteen."

I wiggle my finger at him. "Jailbait. That's what you turning eighteen makes me. And if you kiss me again, I'm calling the cops."

On *Moments of Our Lives*, a woman never calls the cops for help unless the man in question is clearly a Bad Guy, like he kidnapped and raped her sister or works for a crime family in the area. Usually, the two characters will fight and dance around, pretending hostility when really everyone knows that they are perfect for each other. This is not one of those cases. Jackson really is all wrong for me.

I take a different approach. "Jackson, you're going off to college in a few days. It doesn't make sense for you to be hounding me like this."

"I'm not," he says.

"Cornering me outside the bathroom is definitely hounding."

"I'm not going to college." He swallows, Adam's apple bobbing, and brushes his palms against his jeans.

"You're what?" Because all Barbara has talked about since Jackson was twelve was how he would go to college and become a doctor. Jackson talked about becoming a pro baseball player or maybe an astronaut. Although come to think of it, he hasn't talked about the future much in the last year.

"Not going," he clarifies. "Nicaragua, it changed me." He

thumps his chest. "In here. I don't know how to explain it—I just know that college and football, it's not what I want anymore."

Jackson's not winning any points with me. If there was a Rule #6 of the Plan, it would be that He Must Be Able to Hold Down a Job for More Than Three Months. College seems like a good way to assure you're employable as more than a retail clerk. It was the one thing in his favor, as far as I was concerned, and now he's throwing it away?

A hint of the disappointment I feel must show, because he says, "You don't know what I saw down there, Abby. Children living in the streets, begging and starving and sick. Ten- and eleven-year-old-prostitutes selling themselves to middle-aged men? Kids disappear off the streets every day and no one looks for them. I can't go on with my life like that stuff doesn't exist. I have to do something."

"What can you do?" This was a new Jackson to me. Not Jack-Off, Cody's hot big brother, but some new person who had thoughts and opinions I'd never heard.

He shrugs and wipes his hands on his jeans again. "I don't know yet. For now, I'm going to find a job, work, and save up money. I've got a little put away for college, but if I want to go down there for good, I'll need a chunk of change."

"You're going back?"

"Well, yeah. How else can I help?"

Raising money? Petitions? But I don't say it, because I can see he means it and really, it's kind of noble. I suddenly feel bad for resenting my sisters, all the times I got mad when they ate the last Dove bar or wouldn't drive me to the movies when I wanted them to. At least we have a home, food, and a safe place to sleep.

"Does Barbara know?" Because Barbara might think it's all well and good for him to go down there in the summer, but to skip out on college and leave the country indefinitely? It's not the kind of news I'd want to break to her.

Jackson clearly thinks the same. "I'm supposed to leave for A.U. next week. I don't know how to tell her. I'm too late to get any of their deposits and stuff refunded. They'll probably kill me."

If we were on *Passion's Promise*, he could tell her he was going to college but go to Nicaragua instead and have someone send her fake postcards from A.U. Everything would be fine, until another character vacationed in Central America, saw Jackson, and told his mom, and then she'd have the mother of all cows. She would cut him out of her will, and he would die of some unheard-of illness that usually only afflicts actors who ask for a pay raise.

"You won't tell anyone, will you?" Jackson swallows again. "She needs to hear it from me."

"You're not worried about your dad?"

"Naw, he's the one who signed me up for the program. Builds character, he said. Dad might be upset at first, but how can he complain about something that was his idea in the first place?"

"So, you're really not leaving. At least not yet."

"Nope." He grins. "You're stuck with me."

Stuck *on* you is more like it, but just because he's not the total selfish jerk he used to be doesn't mean the other Rules don't apply. "I'd better get back," I say. "Brian must be wondering where I am."

Jackson's face tightens but he nods. "Whatever you say, Abby. But I still think we deserve another chance."

I wiggle my fingers at him in a bye-bye gesture. "Jailbait, Jack-Off. Jailbait."

Chapter 9

When I get back to the living room, the movie is over. Shelby is doing that mom thing where she is oozing herself out of the chair with as little movement as possible so Hannah, asleep on her lap, won't wake up. Everyone is silently watching her awkward gymnastics in a way that makes me think she's threatened them with something horrible to keep them from making noise. Once she's got Hannah out of the room, the chatter starts up.

"Good movie, right?" Gustavo asks, clearly only caring what Kait thinks.

She smiles at him in her slutty way, but I decide it's okay. Gustavo has a lot of the Rules going for him, even #6, Must Be Able to Hold Down a Job for More Than Three Months, which is not officially a Rule. Stephanie is asleep in the sling Kait carries her around in. I hope that if Kait follows through on her slutty-smile promise, she will at least have the decency to leave Stephanie in the living room with me. I can't imagine the hang-ups a person might get from watching Mom do her boss from the crib.

"Pretty good," Kait agrees with Gustavo. "I've seen it before, though. Or maybe it was another movie. Is there more than one?"

Gustavo looks pained. I guess as a movie-store manager, he's something of an expert in the field. All he says, though, is "Yes, three."

"Maybe you can bring the others over tomorrow?" Kait suggests in a way that makes me think Gustavo has already gotten lucky. Eewww, a day out of the hospital and she's already back at it. Is that even physically possible?

"Kait, can you help me?" I hand her a popcorn bowl and nod toward the kitchen. Time for a sister-to-sister chat. As soon as we're alone, I ask, "So soon?"

"What?" She blinks at me in confusion, then comprehension dawns when I point my finger in a little you-and-him gesture. "You think I . . . ? Do you have any idea how sore my nipples are? Come on, Abby, even you should know there's more than one way to satisfy a guy."

Again, eewww. I shouldn't have even asked. But the protectiveness I feel toward Stephanie makes me push ahead. "Even using, um, alternate methods, do you really think that's something you should be doing around Steph?"

"She'll be asleep." Kait stacks the bowl in the sink, then turns and leans against the edge. "Not that this is any of your business."

"How do you know she'll sleep? What if she wakes up, right in the middle of you-know-what?" I pass her some plastic tumblers to add to the pile in the sink.

Kait shrugs and runs some water over the dishes. "The

nurse practitioner told me preemies sleep a lot, and she's right. I actually have to wake her up every four hours for her feedings. Then she drops right back to sleep. Don't worry so much, Abby. Stephanie's an easy baby."

"That's not how it was with Hannah," I remind her. Hannah was a handful from day one.

"She had colic." Shelby joins us in the kitchen, gets a spoon and the ice cream from the freezer, and helps herself to a few bites right out of the carton.

"I'm not saying I'm glad Stephanie was premature, but it's nice that she's so calm." Kait gets her own spoon and digs out a scoop of cookies and cream. "Dr. Patty says that a serene and healthy mom raises a serene and healthy baby. So that's my focus right now. Serene and healthy. It's even more critical with preemies."

Shelby grunts. "Right, premature. Kait, you're not fooling anyone."

Kait freezes, ice cream halfway to her mouth. "What are you talking about?"

Raising one perfectly plucked eyebrow, Shelby says, "If you count backwards nine months from Stephanie's birthday, you end up at Jackson, not Steve."

"No!" It's Kait that says the word, but I'm definitely thinking it. "I know she's Steve's."

"Wanting her to be Steve's is very different from knowing." Shelby licks the back of her spoon and tosses it in the sink. "I'm just saying, better come clean soon. Jackson would be a good dad for her."

"You don't know everything!" Kait yells, and huffs out of

the room, definitely not serene. I saw the tears in her eyes, and a weird knot forms in my stomach.

"Five pounds, eleven ounces is a perfectly normal birth weight for a full-term baby," Shelby tells me. "I looked it up."

I just shake my head at her and leave. It was easier when I thought Shelby was lying, but birth weight is a fact. That Jackson and Kait slept together and Stephanie was born nine months later is a fact. I really don't like how this is all adding up. Jackson, Stephanie's dad? It's so horrible, it just might be true.

Back in the living room, the boys have put on another movie, but it doesn't look like anyone's watching it. Kait is on the couch with Gustavo on the floor in front of her. He's holding Stephanie while Kait gives him a shoulder massage. By the glazed expression on his face and the intense concentration on hers, they certainly have no idea that Indiana Jones is once again in a peck of trouble.

"Brian?" I decide it must be awkward for him to watch my sister put the moves on her boss. Almost as awkward as it is for me to think about just what "other ways to satisfy a guy" means. "Do you want to see the eighth wonder of the world?"

"Right here in Cottonwood?" His eyes lift at the corners when he smiles.

"Mm-hmm, follow me next door." I lead, collecting Cody, and we go out the front and over to Cody's house. I take a left through the family room and a right after the first bathroom.

"My room? That's the big deal?" Cody has not said anything to Brian yet tonight outside of a quick hey when Brian walked in. I guess you could call that good behavior, so he's not technically breaking his promise. He is careful to keep me between them.

I take three strides across the small room. Cody's bed is neatly made, as always, with the navy spread he picked out when he was twelve. His books from school are piled, largest to smallest, on his built-in desk next to his laptop, which is open but sleeping.

Cody tries to distract me by saying, "I've got a whole week of *Passion's Promise* on the DVR. Want to catch a few episodes?"

But it doesn't work. What are Friday afternoons for if not for catching up on all my soaps? "Already seen 'em," I reply.

"And you didn't invite me over?" He tilts his head in that hurt way he has.

"You were pouting," I remind him. Crossing the vaguely Navajo throw rug, I fling open the mirrored closet door. "Ta-da! Have you ever seen anything like it?"

If you watch a lot of reruns of *Swept Clean!* or *Organize Me!* like I do, then you have seen this before. Cody's closet is a marvel of order. Clothes are separated by type, arranged by color from darks to lights, and all hung on black hangers.

"Everything looks good on black," Cody says defensively, like we are going to judge him for his mono-color hangers.

Even more impressive, at least to me, is the shoe organizer with every shoe clean and matched with its mate. Since I share my closet with Kait, and neither one of us is especially concerned with closet cleanliness, finding a matching pair of shoes is like a treasure hunt. Cody has organized and reorganized my closet, but it never lasts.

"Wow," Brian says. "My mom would kill for a closet like that." He kneels down and looks at the bottom row of pants. "Are they arranged by style, too?" Khakis to the left, jeans in the middle, dress pants to the right.

Cody nods, and I could kick him for not talking to Brian.

"Tell him when you did this," I prompt.

For a second, it looks like Cody's not going to answer. Then he says, "Third grade."

"Man," Brian says. "But I guess my closet looks pretty much the same as it did back then, too. A total disaster."

Another thing Brian and I have in common. "Me, too. Cody's helped me a bunch of times, but I guess I don't have the discipline it takes." Or the anal retentiveness, or the cleaning lady who comes every other week to keep the rest of the room under control.

"Thanks for showing me," Brian says. "I think I'm inspired to tame my own closet clutter."

Cody flicks his gaze my way, like I should do something. But what? I know he won't like what I'm going to do next.

"Cody could help you!" I say it like this brilliant idea has just occurred to me. "Maybe this weekend? Cody and I could come over. It'd be just like one of those shows!"

"Like HGTV?" Brian's smile is really big and shows that one tooth is slightly crooked. This guy is so perfectly imperfect I could gag. "Awesome."

"Great." I seal the deal with a handshake. "Your designer, Cody, and his lovely assistant, me, will be glad to reorganize your closet. Hey, we could do before-and-after pictures!"

Brian gets into the idea. "I'll take the before pics tonight,

and you guys can come over tomorrow. This will be perfect."
His smile is for Cody, but Cody is looking out the window. His
eyes are big.

"What is it?" The view from Cody's room is of my driveway.

"Steve's home."

I rush to the window and jerk the blinds up and out of my
way. Sure enough, the Guitar Player is in the driveway already
getting into it with Mom. There is a tall, model-thin woman
next to him. She must be the Guitar Groupie he stayed with
when Kait was in the hospital. They are standing in front of a
new Ford Focus. My first thought is how did she bend all that
leg into such a tiny car? My second thought is I better get home
right now. Because Mom was willing to buy the "She's just a
friend" line over the phone, but it looks like now that they've
met in person, things are not all happy in Newlywed Land.

It's dark, but that too-bright streetlight in front of our house
illuminates the scene perfectly. The Guitar Player, motionless
between the Groupie and my mom. The Groupie's jaw chomp-
ing up and down on a piece of gum.

The Guitar Player's voice floats from the driveway and
through Cody's open window. "Mona, I swear it didn't mean
anything."

And to make things worse, a loud baby wail from my bedroom announces that Kait and Stephanie are watching it all
from our window.

Kait flings open the window and holds Stephanie up.
"Steve, look at our daughter! Isn't she beautiful?"

Steve swivels his head around, and Kait actually dangles
Stephanie out the window. Gustavo is behind her, engaged in a

bit of careful wrestling to get the baby back into the room, but Kait won't be budged.

I stick my own head out Cody's window and scream, "Kait, get the baby inside *now!*"

She reels Stephanie back in. The Guitar Player's head swings from the window, to the Groupie, to my mom.

"You said it was over with her," the Groupie says, snapping her gum. Whether she means Mom or Kait or both is unclear.

"Over?" Mom shouts, hands clenching at her sides. "You bet it's over!"

Mrs. Duran from across the street comes outside with a watering can. Only she doesn't water any of her dying flowers, just stands in the drive and stares. The Guitar Player shouts something, then Mom yells back. Kait is crying and Stephanie lets out a scream loud enough to wake the whole neighborhood.

"I'd better get over there," I say to the guys. "Sorry you have to see this, Brian."

"No, it's fine." He has that look in his eyes that explains exactly why *Jerry Springer* has been on the air for so long. Who doesn't like a nice white-trash scuffle now and then?

Cody hugs me before I go. "Come over later if you need to. You can sleep here."

"I know." It wouldn't be the first time I'd hidden at Cody's. I rest my chin on his shoulder and whisper, "Cody, give Brian a chance, will you? He seems so nice."

Cody steps back, shoves me away from him. "What? What did you say to me?"

"I was trying to be discreet." I look meaningfully in Brian's direction. Brian is politely pretending not to pay attention, standing in front of Cody's bookcase with his attention fixed on the collection of Little League trophies across the top.

"I am not gay." Cody's voice is low, but then he says it again louder. "I am not gay."

Brian's head whips around. I feel like I'm going to cry because I've never seen Cody look at me like this. Cold, flat. Like I'm no one to him.

"I . . . I didn't mean . . ."

"You! You know I'm not! Say it, Abby."

"You're not gay. Okay, Cody, you're not. I'm sorry." Tears stream down my cheeks, but unlike the rest of my family, when I'm upset I get quieter, not louder. "Don't be mad," I whisper.

"Get out." He points to the open door. He's talking to me, but his eyes are on Brian. The coldness I see in him stutters my heart. It beats overtime, like a drummer on speed, when Cody says in his dead-serious way, "Abigail Elizabeth Savage, don't bother coming back."

Brian leaves through the door but I slip out the window, slide across the ledge, and land on the sandy ground. I wonder if what I've done is unforgivable.

Brian walks down to the street, where his car is parked. I catch up to him. Over the shouting in the driveway, I say, "I'm sorry."

"It's harder for some guys than others. Don't worry about it."

"I'll still help you with your closet."

The smile he gives me is a dull version of the real thing. "Forget about it. I'd never be able to keep it clean anyway."

He drives away and I turn to face my family. Still outside, still yelling. Now it has escalated to the point where no one is taking turns. They are all shouting or crying, and waving their hands around. Mrs. Duran has been joined by her husband, and they appear to be enjoying the show.

I put on my sternest face. I reach deep inside for the voice I use when Hannah is about to do something life-threatening and I bellow, "Everyone! In the house! Now!"

Chapter ♥ 10

Inside, Jackson sits at the kitchen table, eating our leftover pizza from last night.

"Make yourself at home," I snap, and collapse into the chair across from him. Although I was quite clear that they should all come inside, I can still hear them yelling at each other in the yard. My Hannah voice was not enough to penetrate their white-trash-fighting-on-the-lawn haze.

Jackson holds out a piece of cold pizza for me. "You get some alone time with *Bri-an*?"

"No." What I got was a big ol' fight with Cody, but I'm not telling Jackson about any of it. I take a big bite of cold pineapple bits and congealed cheese. Yum. "I hate them. All of them."

"Who?"

"My psycho family. Can't you hear them?"

"I learned to tune out the Savage quarrels years ago. What's this one about?"

That my family has had it out on the front lawn many a time before is no neighborhood secret. "I'm not sure. The Guitar Player's back with some bimbo, and Kait's pushing the baby out the window at him."

"So *Savage*." He fake shudders.

I pick off a hunk of pineapple and toss it at him. He bobs his head and catches it in his mouth. "Thanks."

I contemplate throwing other, heavier, and more damaging things at him. Like the toaster. I could reach it from here.

Before I can act, Shelby walks in with Hannah on her hip. "What's the racket?"

"Same old, same old," Jackson says. "Want a slice?"

Shelby arranges a surprisingly compliant Hannah on a chair with a phone book under her. This brings her up so we can see her eyes and tip of her nose over the top of the table. It's weird to see our mom's eyes staring out of her chubby face.

"No, thanks. I'm gonna make Hannah a late-night snack and then it's straight back to sleep—right, young lady?"

Hannah nods like a good girl, her razored bangs playing peek-a-boo with her eyebrows. Very suspicious. Bribery must be involved.

Shelby opens the freezer and looks in the door where we usually keep the ice cream. It's empty. She pushes things aside, rearranges the frozen orange juice concentrate and the Ziploc bags of who-knows-what. No ice cream.

"Abs?" Shelby speaks very slowly. "Do you know where *it* is?"

"The ice cream?" I say, because I don't think you should bribe three-year-olds into going to bed with a bowl of ice cream. It's not like Shelby has dental insurance.

Hannah's upper lip starts to quiver. Shelby sees it and searches more frantically through the freezer, shoving aside frozen peas and long-forgotten vegetable-medley packs. "Abs? A little help here?"

"Why would I know?"

Hannah whimpers.

"Abs, please. I haven't slept in three nights. Please, please tell me there is ice cream in this freezer. It was here earlier tonight—why can't I find it?"

Jackson moves his gaze from Shelby to me like it's Wimbledon. His face is too carefully blank. I get up and look in the sink. Unrinsed ice-cream bowl.

"Ask Jackson," I say.

He gives Shelby his heartbreaker smile. The one he tried with me when he said, "Yes, it's technically possible that I'm the father."

"You can't expect a man to resist cookies and cream." He smacks his lips.

Shelby, who to my knowledge has not slept with Jackson but is obviously trying to rectify that situation, lights up. She pouts her full lip-glossed lips at him. "Jackson, I promised the baby some ice cream. Now what am I gonna do?"

On cue, Hannah lets out one of her patented howls. It goes on and on, like the fire alarm at school.

"Please?" Shelby does her shy smile, the one that tricks boys into thinking she's a sweet *thang* when she really is a manipulative *thang*.

But it works, like it always does. Sometimes I think I was born without that special gene my sisters have. The gene that lets them know just what to say to get a guy to do anything they want.

Jackson stands and pushes in his chair. "Be right back, honey." I think he's talking to Hannah, but I'm not sure. Hannah isn't clear either, because her howl kicks up a notch, not high enough that only dogs can hear but close.

I cover my ears. "Comin' with, Romeo. I can't stand another second of this." Jackson and I head down the hallway. As Hannah's howls lower in volume, the fight outside becomes audible again.

"Tubes tied, my ass!" the Guitar Player is shouting at Mom. "You lied then and you're probably lying now!"

"Yeah!" says the Guitar Groupie, hands on her hips.

Is that the sound of hair being ripped out of a head? No. We pass by them on the way to the car and I see that it's just the Guitar Groupie's too-tight shirt my mom has grabbed in her fist. The material in the back gives way, tearing apart to show there's no bra underneath.

Mom sees me then. Lets go and says in a voice that I'm sure they can hear on the other side of Mingus Mountain, "Oh, Abby, if you go by the store, get me some laxatives, will you? I haven't taken a decent crap in days."

Mom lays into the Groupie again, the Guitar Player stepping between them like a referee in a prizefight gone bad. I cannot catch a break tonight. Not one.

Mrs. Duran doesn't have much of a lawn—mostly sand and a few surviving patches of a grass that Mr. Duran is forced to mow once a month—but apparently it's quite the hot spot this evening. It only takes a few minutes to get to Jackson's car, but in that time, neighbors from up and down the street have gathered and are watching while my mom hangs on to the Guitar

Player's sleeve, begging him not to go off with that "piece of trash! I'm telling you she's no good for you! Come inside and I'll show you what you've been missing all these nights away!"

Mr. Ketchum, from three houses down, brings a lawn chair and sets it up in front of Mrs. Duran's house. Mr. Duran comes out of their house with a cooler. Some of the neighbors help themselves to a beer.

Piece of Trash Groupie tugs on the Guitar Player's other arm. "Steve, she's crazy. It's not safe to leave you here." She pouts her clearly collagen-injected lips at him.

The neighbors appear to be debating the truth of her statement.

Kait pops her head out the window. "Steve, when are you coming in to see our new baby? Steve?"

I close my eyes against the pain. Can you die of embarrassment? If the barrel cactus in our front yard was healthier, perhaps I could impale myself on it and put myself out of this misery. Sadly, the cactus would most likely just collapse under my weight.

"Get me out of here," I say to Jackson.

"My dream come true." He takes my elbow and guides me over to his driveway. Distance in no way keeps me from hearing my mother say, "Steve, no other woman can make you feel the way I do!"

Jackson hits his forehead with his palm. "Sorry, I'm confused. In the dream, you say, 'Get me out of *these*.'" He points to my jeans.

I slap at his finger. "Don't make me beg."

"Hmm," he says as he opens the door for me and then goes to his side of the car. "Begging? Now that's an interesting thought."

I try not to smile. "Don't think you can cheer me up. You can't."

"Wouldn't dream of it." He backs onto the road, and we leave my still-arguing family behind.

The nearest grocery store is sixteen miles down Highway 260, so I flick on the radio. Jackson immediately turns it off.

"Abby, tell me what's wrong."

"Nothing, and I liked that song." Even though I don't remember what it was. Could've been a commercial jingle for all I know.

"I can tell you're upset about something."

Besides the idea of you and my sister being parents together? But I don't want to touch that with a ten-foot pole tonight. How about, *I accidentally outed your brother and now he hates me forever?* Nope, not that, either. I fall back on an old standard. "You saw them. Putting on a show for the whole neighborhood. I don't know why they're like that."

Jackson shakes his head. "That's not it. You're used to them. This is something new."

I fix my gaze out the side window. Mountains in the distance, cacti arms upraised in the pools of light spread by the streetlights we pass.

"It's that big, huh? Let me guess—you're pregnant!"

"No!" For that, I hit his arm. Hard. "Not even."

Jackson seems not to notice the killing blow I gave him. "Must be Cody then."

"Why do you say that?"

"Because if it wasn't him, you'd have already told him the problem and you wouldn't be upset anymore. So what happened? He doesn't like you being with Brian?"

It's true I have lots of things to be upset about, and Cody is definitely one of them. The whole situation is so messy, I'm not sure where to start or even if I should. Because Cody wouldn't want his big brother in his business, and as long as Jackson thinks I'm interested in Brian, maybe he'll back off. But I keep seeing that expression on Cody's face, how he looked at me like I was a stranger, or worse, one of the guys at school who's been taunting him.

We stop at a red light. Jackson turns his head toward me, takes his hand off the wheel, and pats my knee. "Come on now, honey, tell Jackson what's on your mind."

The light turns green. We surge ahead. I look at Jackson's profile, the line of his jaw and the way his nose turns up ever so slightly at the end. He must at least suspect. He's known Cody even longer than I have.

"You know how those kids at school have been harassing Cody?"

Jackson's lips tighten. "Yeah."

"You know what it's about?"

"Yeah."

"So, I just thought Brian was a really nice guy, and I told Cody to give him a chance but he got mad at me. Really mad." I'm pleased at how well Jackson is taking this. It's like we're on the same page, completely in sync with each other's thoughts.

"So Cody doesn't like you hanging around Brian." Jackson

nods like it all makes sense to him, which is not the page I'm on at all.

"No, it's . . . Well, I think Brian's gay. So I told Cody to take a chance."

"Cody? My brother?"

Uh-oh, this isn't going well. "Yeah, you know, because he's . . . I mean, I thought he was . . ."

"*That's* why they're teasing him at school? My brother's gay?" He pulls off the road, jams on the parking brake. "I thought it was because of what happened at Hell Week his freshman year. How he got cut from football. With me as his big brother . . . I mean, it was pretty humiliating."

"Nope. He's gay. At least, I think so."

Jackson bangs his forehead against the steering wheel. "Of course he is." *Bang.* "Of course." *Bang.* "My brother." *Bang.* He's off a few inches on the last *bang*, and the horn honks loudly.

He rolls his head so he can see me. "Cody told you?"

"Not exactly. I just know. Or I thought I did. He says he's not."

"He's not?"

"He says he's not. I think because of all the stuff at school."

Jackson's head rolls the other way. He lifts it an inch. "I should've seen it sooner." *Bang.* His eyes squeeze shut. "Do my parents know?"

I shrug, then realize he can't see me. "How could they?"

"Do you have any idea how they would take this?" *Bang.* "It's all making sense."

"What?"

Jackson looks at me, those deep blue eyes searching my

face. "I couldn't figure out why he wasn't in love with you. When I asked, he was shocked. All I could think was how can he spend so much time with you and not want to be with you? Now I know. God, I wish I didn't."

I'm not sure what to say. If this was *Moments of Our Lives*, we'd crash in the car or one of us would have a seizure right now. But our car's not moving and neither one of us appears to be seizure prone. Instead, we sit silently and watch the flow of traffic pass us by.

At the Fry's, we stand in the frozen-food aisle. Jackson holds the door open and the glass frosts over.

"Cookies and cream? Or something else?"

When I don't respond, he grabs two cartons and puts them in the cart. As we roll along, I decide that since Jackson's paying, we need a few other things. I add a frozen pizza and toaster waffles to the basket.

"That's fair," Jackson says as if a few extra dollars will make up for the years he's helped himself to our fridge. I pick up some tater tots and french fries and stick them beside the ice cream. I don't forget the laxatives, but I don't buy them, either. Touch those things? In front of Jackson? No way.

We roll from aisle to aisle through the busy store. Moms shop with their kids in tow, an older guy hums along in one of those complimentary Fry's motorized scooter-carts. There's a near collision when he rounds a corner and almost takes out a Tostitos display. I toss a few more things in our basket—you can never have too much salsa—and we head for the checkout line.

"You know," Jackson says thoughtfully as we stroll through the bakery, "I should've known earlier. I mean, he's really good at sports, but he gets himself cut from football? And I remember there was this girl last year always calling our house, and he made me say he wasn't home."

What girl? But I decide to let it go. Now that Jackson's on board with the whole gay thing, he seems to be shuffling through memories, looking for evidence. So I don't tell him that Cody botched his football tryouts because he didn't want to be on the same team with Jackson. I don't say that Jackson stuffing Cody's clothes in the locker-room garbage during Hell Week, forcing him to walk naked in front of the other players, was the reason he quit. Plenty of time later to pile on that kind of guilt.

We are standing behind a woman with three kids, all under the age of five, when I see my favorite soap magazine. Since her groceries overflow the cart and the middle kid keeps trying to slip chocolate bars off the rack and into his mouth, I figure we'll be here awhile. I'm flipping through *Soap Digest*, scanning for pics of my favorite daytime hunks—especially Paul from *Veterans' Hospital*—when I get sucked into an article about what's coming up on *Veterans' Hospital*. Poor Paul. Malibu, his new wife, isn't really pregnant at all. But his ex-girlfriend Cari is. Only what no one's telling Paul is that Malibu and Cari have a secret plan. And that's when it hits me. The explanation for everything. Baby swap.

Chapter ♥ 11

Clearly, there was a huge mix-up when I was born. My real parents have no idea they are raising Mona's wild child. They probably wonder how such a nice family ended up with such a promiscuous, low-class daughter. If only they knew.

Jackson rams me with the cart, and I take a few steps forward in line. I pick up another soap magazine and scan the contents carefully for any other story lines involving baby swaps that might explain what happened to me. Unfortunately, a test-tube mix-up is unlikely since there's no way my mom ever had enough money for fertility treatments. Or that she'd even go through the trouble when she already had two kids. The most likely scenario has got to be mislabeling in the nursery. If only I could figure out how to prove it.

Jackson pays for the food and we are on our way. We load the groceries into the trunk in silence, climb into the car, and pull out of the parking lot. We are not talking about Cody. We are not talking about my baby-swap theory. Basically, we are not talking. It feels weird. Jackson and I have never been at a loss for words. Usually insulting words, but never has a silence stretched so long between us.

"What's wrong?" I ask, reversing our roles. Hey, if he can be sensitive, so can I.

"I can't stop thinking about my brother. You know I always thought he was too uptight to be much fun, but when I was in Nicaragua I missed him. Really missed him. I didn't realize how much I like joking around with him, complaining about our parents, all the stuff I took for granted. But for all that, it's like I don't really know him."

I remember Cody's cold look. How can someone so familiar become a stranger over a few words?

"Maybe I'm wrong," I say, words that rarely come out of my mouth. "Maybe he is straight."

"I don't know." Jackson shakes his shaggy head. "It kind of makes sense."

Another silence. I decide to tell him my baby-swap idea. He laughs so hard I'm worried he'll pop a blood vessel.

"Abby," he says, "there's only one family passing out bodies like yours."

It's true that my sisters and I are pretty good eye candy, but it's not impossible that another family could have equally attractive genes. When I tell Jackson this, he says, "Now, if you weren't sure your dad was your dad, that I'd believe in a heartbeat. But you look too much like your mom to think you were swapped at birth."

My dad not my dad? Why hadn't it occurred to me before? It wasn't like either one of my parents was particularly good at being faithful.

"Thanks, Jackson, you really know how to cheer a girl up!" There's nothing better than thinking you might have a secret parent out there, about to swoop in and inform you that you're really a princess of a small European country. At least, that's what happened to Charity on *Veterans' Hospital*. Why shouldn't it happen to me, too? I smile and switch on the radio, hoping to find an upbeat song.

Jackson sings along, no matter what station I tune in, and it's the first time I find out how diverse his musical tastes are. From Shakira's latest to some old-school Beastie Boys, he knows them all. He even sings along to that old Sinatra song "Fly Me to the Moon" that I find on the oldies station. It's way too endearing. I've got to get out of this quicksand of cuteness. And I know just the thing to think about.

I watch Jackson from the corner of my eye. Does Stephanie look like him? Is that her nose on his face? Did she get her wispy hair from the Jennings side of the family? I should just ask him again, but I can't quite bring myself to say the words. *Stick to the Rules, Abby, and none of this will matter.*

Jackson drops me off at my house and reminds me to take both grocery bags. He makes some comment about how my family's taken it inside now, and I see that he's right. We can hear them through the open windows, but at least the crowd on the street has dispersed. He gives me a casual "Later" and doesn't say anything annoying. Or provocative. Isn't this exactly how I wanted it between us? I should be happy that he drives away without looking back. But I'm not.

Hannah is already asleep when I get home with the ice cream. I cram all the frozen goods into the freezer but keep one of the Breyers tubs out.

"You want some?" I ask Shelby, who is at the kitchen table, braiding her hair into a complicated fishtail.

"I'm still trying to lose this baby weight." Shelby frowns at her imagined belly. If anything, she's smaller than before she had Hannah. Chasing after a toddler can really take off the pounds. Besides, she eats like a jackrabbit: veggies and water 24/7. That she'd had a few spoonfuls of ice cream earlier tonight means she probably won't eat breakfast tomorrow.

But I guess the three sleepless nights have gotten to her, because Shelby surprises me when she lets me make her a bowl, half a scoop with some chocolate syrup on the side. She's too tired to even say something snippy about why Jackson and I were gone so long, an opportunity she wouldn't usually pass up. I dish myself two scoops, no chocolate.

"What happened with Mom and the Guitar Player?" I ask between mouthfuls of cookies and cream.

Shelby is about to answer when I hear Mom's cries from the bedroom. And not cries of pain or sadness, either. Something I learned when Shelby was pregnant is that no, sex does not hurt the baby.

"So all's well then," I say.

"Abs, can you do me a huge favor?"

Huge favors always involve Hannah, but since it's not like Cody and I will be hanging out this weekend, I agree. And am immediately sorry.

"Great, because Dean—he's the new guy at my work, remember?—wants to take me away for the weekend. To Sedona! Isn't that romantic? We're going to do some kind of rock therapy."

"Stone," I correct her, thinking how Mom is getting her rock therapy right now from the Guitar Player.

I lick the last of the ice cream from my spoon and dump the bowl in the sink. Maybe the dish fairies will come tonight. Or more likely, I'll get stuck doing them tomorrow.

"Good night. I'll need all the sleep I can get if I'm watching Hannah this weekend."

I slip quietly into my room, careful not to wake Kait or Stephanie. In the closet, I shimmy out of my clothes and into pj's. Stephanie's small face is illuminated by the streetlight outside our window. She is so pink and tiny that I have to bend down and kiss her wispy hair. Stephanie doesn't stir and I worry that if she really is a premie, can I trust Kait to remember the feeding schedule? Maybe I should have Cody make us a spreadsheet or something. But then I remember that Cody won't be doing anything for me for a while and I hope it's not too long before I can figure out a way to get him to forgive me.

When I stand up, I'm greeted by a full moon. Not the kind that hangs in the sky at night. Gustavo is asleep with his arms wrapped around my sister. Since it's a twin bed, his naked butt hangs off the edge, peeking out from under the sheet for all the world to see. Or at least for me and Stephanie to see. I think about what else Stephanie might've seen tonight. I hope she's not scarred for life.

Saturday morning. I wake up when Shelby dumps Hannah on top of me in bed.

"Wakey, wakey!" she calls in her singsong baby voice.

I moan and roll over. Hannah giggles and sticks a finger in my mouth. It tastes like something besides skin. I'm not sure what, and I probably don't want to know. I squint in the direction of the crib. Stephanie's blue eyes are open and watching me. They look so much like Jackson's that for a second I forget blue eyes run in my family, too, and that it's also true some babies change eye color as they get older. Right now she's Jackson-blue, and it makes me want to hit something.

"Dean's here." Shelby shoves at me. "I'm leaving, so get up. Hannah hasn't had breakfast yet."

Of course she hasn't. I sit up. Gustavo's ass is still hanging off the edge of the bed. Shelby's gaze follows mine and she cracks up.

"Perfect, that's just perfect!" she laughs. She yanks the sheet off Kait's bed. Kait's in a baggy black T-shirt and pink undies, but Gustavo is completely naked. Shelby laughs so hard a booger flies out one nostril.

"Oh!" Her hand flies to cover her nose and mouth, and she runs out of the room.

Hannah is getting pretty heavy for such a little thing, so I don't move fast enough when Kait throws her pillow at me.

"Perv!" she accuses.

"I'm not the one with a naked boss in my bed. Besides, it was Shelby."

"Huh?" Gustavo mumbles, and I see that even nude, his hair is still in that ponytail holder. Either wear it down or cut it off, bud.

I don't usually drink coffee in the morning, but I can tell that today I'm going to need all the help I can get.

After breakfast, Hannah and I are playing her favorite game—take all the pots out of the bottom cupboard and bang them together—when there is a knock on the door. Since I'm the reluctant babysitter and there are at least three other people in the house, I let someone else get it.

I am not expecting it to be Cody, but he squats down next to Hannah and says, "Hey."

"Thas my bang bang!" Hannah points at our spaghetti pot and laughs maniacally.

Cody grins at her. "I see. What about that one?" He points to a strainer.

"Mine!" she announces, picking up a wooden spoon and whacking it on a frying pan.

"How are you?" I ask Cody at the same time he says, "Can we talk for a minute?"

"It's probably quieter in the living room." Hannah howls when I get up, so I take down the most forbidden—and therefore most fun—of all the non-lethal kitchen accessories. The whisk. Hannah squeals with delight, grabs it from me, and promptly gets her chubby fingers stuck in the wires.

"That'll keep her busy for a while," I say, and go with Cody into the next room. There are still pillows on the floor from last night and a few tumblers and a popcorn bowl on the glass coffee table that no one bothered to take to the kitchen. I sit on one of the floor pillows and angle it so I can see through the archway and into the kitchen. Hannah is gnawing on the whisk like a dog with a fresh T-bone. "What's up?"

Cody sits across from me, absently picking tiny bits of popcorn from between the wooden planks of the floor. "We've never had a fight before," he says.

"What about the Great Halloween Fight of Fifth Grade?" I remind him. I wanted to be a princess. He wanted us to dress up like superheroes. We didn't speak for almost ten minutes. That argument was solved when Mom informed me I'd be the same thing I was every year—something you can make out of a sheet. So, Cody went as Spider-Man and I was Static Cling. Picture a pink-flowered sheet with socks safety-pinned all over.

"I liked your costume," Cody says now, obviously not the one who had to explain his costume over and over again. "You got lots of candy."

"Yeah, pity candy. Poor little girl wearing her family's laundry around the neighborhood."

Cody laughs and I start to get the feeling that he's forgiven me. He must see the question in my eyes, because he says, "Abby, I'm sorry I was a jerk yesterday."

I thought about this a lot last night, staring at the pale moon of Gustavo's butt. "No, I'm sorry. I shouldn't have said what I did. I was way off base."

"Not totally." He looks at me with his hazel Cody eyes, and

I see the guy next door but also something else. Something older and sadder.

"What is it, Cody?" I can't stand that I made him sad, can't stand that things aren't how they've always been between us. I feel like I'm going to cry.

He picks at the floor some more, then slowly raises his gaze to mine. "What you said yesterday, what you think about me, it's true."

I'm stunned. I mean, I *knew*, but I didn't *know*. I guess I'm silent too long, because Cody stops waiting.

"Jackson talked to me last night. About you and, well . . . everything. I told him. And once I told him, and it felt so good to finally say it, I knew I had to apologize to you. Jackson said it's proof of how close we are that you knew without me telling. He's right. Abby, you're my best friend. Please don't be mad at me."

Now I really am crying, tears leaking like the faucet in the bathroom that the Guitar Player promised to fix and hasn't. I lean forward and wrap Cody in a tight hug. "I'm sorry, Cody. I should've let you do it in your own time."

"My own time would be, um, never. But please don't tell anyone else. This is between you and me, Abs. And Jackson." He pauses, rubbing my back with one hand. "I still can't quite get over that you told Jackson. *Jackson*, of all people. You think I can trust him?"

Trust Jack-Off? No. But Jackson, I'm gonna save the poor children of the world? I nod into Cody's neck.

A loud screech, the kind Hannah lets out when she is hurt,

pierces the air. I scramble to my feet and run to the kitchen.

"Hannah! What have you done?"

She somehow managed to climb up the cupboard door and over into the sink. Her hand is caught in the drain. Thank God the compactor switch is far out of her reach. "Hang on, baby," I say, gently extracting her arm from danger. She calms down to a whimper and inspects her hand carefully once it's free.

I scoop her up and deposit her back on the floor. "Crisis three hundred avoided for the day."

Cody wipes his own wet eyes with the back of one hand. "You'll come to dinner tonight, won't you? Now that Jackson's back, Mom's starting up the Saturday-night tradition again. She's making your favorite."

Since my favorite is anything that wasn't frozen first, he's not exactly narrowing down the menu. I agree anyway, because Saturday-night dinners at Cody's house are like a peek into another world. A normal world.

"It's okay if I bring the baby?"

Cody nods. "You mean Hannah? Because technically she's not the baby anymore."

Hannah looks up from her important work of unscrewing the handle off the soup pot. "I the baby!"

Cody crouches down in front of her. "You're Hannah the big girl now. Stephanie's the baby."

"I the baby!" She makes her point by slamming the pot on his foot. "I the baby!"

Cody backs up, out of pot range, and rubs his toes. "Point taken, Hannah."

I laugh and walk Cody to the door. "I'll try to wear her out today. Maybe she'll sleep through dinner."

Cody is halfway out the door when he stops and turns. "I really did think Brian was perfect for you."

"Except for the whole gay thing, he was. You could call him up. See if he still wants help with his closet."

"That ship's already sailed." The door swings shut behind him.

I'm not so sure he's right. I decide to ask Jackson his opinion on the situation later today. Then I get mad. Since when is Jackson my go-to guy? Ridiculous. I'll call Brian myself and get it straight, so to speak, from the horse's mouth.

Chapter ♥ 12

"Get over here now!" Even though it's only been about three hours since we saw each other, Cody's voice on the phone is urgent. It's unusual for him to be the one with the emergency, so I scoop up Hannah and race next door.

Cody and his parents are standing outside. Walt's dressed like it's not ninety degrees outside, in jeans and a long-sleeved button-down. Sweat plasters the shirt to his back. Barbara's dressed for her daily three-mile walk in comfortable sneakers, running shorts, and a baggy T-shirt.

"Look!" Cody commands. His sandaled feet bounce on the concrete of their front walkway. "Can you believe it?"

There are three cars in the driveway. The LeSabre, the Camry, and a new Accord. Jackson's Corolla is nowhere in sight. He must be out doing whatever it is not-going-to-college guys do on the weekend.

"Hannah, look!" I say after adding up the new Accord and the pure joy on Cody's face. "It's Cody's new car!" I jostle her on my hip in a mini happy dance. She giggles and tangles her fingers in my hair.

"Isn't it great?" Cody hugs his mom first, then his dad. "You two are the best."

Barbara and Walt beam at Cody. "We're so proud of you, son. We know you'll take good care of her," says Walt. He dangles the keys in front of Cody. "Want to take her for a spin?"

"Yes!" I squeal, before realizing Cody probably doesn't have a car seat for Hannah. Shelby doesn't care if Hannah rides along on someone's lap, but there's no way Barbara will let us get away with it. Bummer. I deposit my niece on the ground and frown.

"Without my license? I can't take the test until my birthday next Thursday." Cody clearly wants to snatch those keys out of Walt's hand, but he manages to hold himself back.

Walt winks at him. "What the Motor Vehicle Division doesn't know won't hurt 'em."

This is a humongous thing. Cody's parents are usually sticklers for stuff like rules and laws. I watch Walt and Barbara carefully for any signs that they've had personality transplants. It's rare even on soaps, but it does happen.

Cody's so fast, the movement is like a blur. He holds the keys in front of my nose and swings them back and forth. "Wanna come along?"

"Sorry." I pat Hannah's head. "Babysitting duty."

Barbara holds out her arms. "I've got her, Abby. You two take a quick drive around the block."

She tickles Hannah, and Walt gives a few last-minute directions about using the sideview mirrors. I run to the passenger side of the Accord. Cody opens the Camry door.

"What?" The Camry is Barbara's car.

Cody laughs. "You think they gave *me* the new car? That's Mom's. They went to the dealership this morning to pick it out. I get her old one."

I am a little disappointed on Cody's behalf—what with double whammy of a used car that is not a convertible—but he's so happy, sliding into the driver's seat, that I let it go. At least he has a car. No more awkward drives to and from school with Jackson as our chauffeur.

Climbing in the passenger's side, I inhale that old-car smell covered up by the strong scent of citrus. Maybe it's lemon or lime. It's hard to tell by the shape of the air freshener exactly what it's supposed to be. Cody backs up and smoothly pulls us onto the street.

"This is so cool!" He puts the car in drive and slowly accelerates. Very slowly.

"Speed limit's twenty-five," I say helpfully. "You can probably go thirty with no problem."

"I'm not taking any chances." He keeps the car at fifteen miles per hour. Little girls zoom past us on their bikes. I'm not kidding.

"If you're going to drive like this every day, we're going to have to leave an hour earlier for school. Maybe more."

"Why don't we take your car instead?" His eyes never leave the road.

Ouch. "You're a great driver," I say, patting his leg. "The best. My fave."

Stopped at the last intersection before we turn back onto our own street, Cody yields the right of way to an SUV. He turns his head to check his blind spot. His collar slips down, and I see the faintest outline where his hickey used to be.

"When are you going to tell me who gave you that thing?" Since no new ones have appeared on his body, at least not where I can see them, I assume that whatever happened is over. But I still want to know.

He uses his palm to cover his neck. "I told you, no one."

"It's pretty hard to give yourself one, at least in that location."

He doesn't answer for a long moment. His jaw flexes like he's about to speak, then he shakes his head. "I don't want to tell you."

My throat feels as dry as if I'd scooped up a handful of desert sand and choked it down. "Cody? It can't be that bad."

"I don't want you to hate me. I know you think I'm . . . you know."

Didn't he just come out to me this morning? Was it a dream? Because he's acting like we never talked.

"Be straight with me," I say, and immediately regret my word choice. "What you told me earlier is between you and me. Just like the big secret of where the hickey came from will be. You know you want to tell me. Come on."

Cody tugs on his ear and grinds his teeth. When he turns my way, his eyes are filled with tears. "What's wrong with me, Abby? Why can't I be in love with you? Then everything would be so easy." A single tear escapes, sliding down his nose and into the corner of his mouth.

Being strapped into the bucket seats makes it impossible to get closer. I reach out my hand and lay it on his back.

"Cody, you are who you are. I love you no matter what. You know that, right? There's nothing you could say that would make me hate you."

He takes a deep breath. My hand is trapped between his body and the seat, but I don't move it.

"Abby?" He touches the hickey. "After I found that dildo, I panicked. I can't go through the same thing again this year. So, there's this freshman in my art class. Really cute. I thought, maybe I don't know for sure. Maybe it's all in my head. She'd been flirting with me, so I convinced her to meet me out by the freshman lockers. You know the place?"

"Yeah." There's an alcove between the language-arts building and the lockers that's well known as a hookup place. Last year's senior class wanted to install a condom machine in the alcove as the class gift. Obviously, the principal vetoed that idea and they donated some new software to the computer lab instead.

Cody takes another breath and continues. "We made out. It was stupid—I should never have been there."

"Was it horrible?" I don't know what it's like to be gay, but I was forced to kiss a guy I didn't like at a party last year, thanks to a stupid drinking game, and I can still remember how wrong it felt.

"She's nice. It wasn't her fault." Which is just like Cody, to take all the blame himself. "It's me."

A car stuck behind us honks.

"Why don't you pull over?" I suggest. He doesn't need to be dealing with traffic at a time like this. He sits forward and I get my hand back. We cross the intersection and pull off onto the dirt shoulder.

I take Cody's hand in both of mine and lay my cheek against it. "Everything's going to be okay, Cody. I promise."

He lets out a coughing sound and bends forward. I let go of his hand, unlock my seat belt, and push myself over the middle console as best I can. We are awkwardly arranged, my knee on the armrest, head resting on his back. He chokes back his tears, holding them in, until finally his body relaxes.

I return to my seat. "I love you, Cody." It's the only thing I can think of, the only true thing I know.

He gives me a weak smile. "Love you, too, Abs."

"And don't worry. I won't say anything to anyone." I stare into his eyes so he'll see that I mean what I say.

"Thanks." Reaching over, he laces his fingers with mine. Smiles. "You're the best."

"I know." We sit in silence for a while. His breathing returns to normal. Our hands start to sweat without the A/C. "We going home or what?" I ask.

He starts up the car. "Once more around?"

"Sure." We both need the recovery time. He turns on the radio and we listen to the familiar commercials, watch our neighborhood go by, see the same sights we've been looking at our whole lives, and I realize that nothing is really the same. Not anymore.

After we've circled the block five times, Cody pulls back into his driveway. Hannah is sitting on their lawn, which, typical of our desert climate, is mostly sand and rock, with a few out-croppings of strategically placed cactus. She's about to put something in her mouth. It wiggles, which means it's still alive. I read that bug eating is a phase, but I'm beginning to think she's never going to outgrow it.

Barbara is not paying attention, saying something to Walt with her hand on his arm.

I leap out of the car. "Hannah, no!" But I'm too late. The whatever-it-was disappears into her mouth.

"Oh, Hannah." I wedge my finger in her mouth, trying to get her to spit it out, but I'm too late. She swallows it.

"You've got to watch her every second," I snap, before remembering that I'm talking to Barbara Super Mom and that Hannah isn't really her responsibility and that Cody and I were gone a lot longer than we were supposed to be.

"Must be one fun block. I'm surprised you didn't get dizzy going around so many times," Walt says, smiling and patting Cody's back. "How's she handle, son?"

Cody looks completely himself now. "Great, Dad. It's perfect."

"Not a bad deal for me, either," Barbara says, tactfully ignoring my earlier statement. "I've been wanting a new car for years. I'm just so glad we finally had the time to take care of this today." She smiles at Walt.

I pick Hannah up, hands under her armpits, and she wraps her chunky legs around my waist. "We'd better get going. Cody, you coming to get me for dinner or what?"

He laughs. "Sorry, princess. I'm not wasting gas driving from my house to yours."

With Hannah settled on my hip, I turn to Barbara. "Is there

anything I can bring tonight?" It's not something my family would ever think of, but I've noticed that Barbara always brings something to our pig roasts and barbecues.

She looks surprised by my request, but in a good way. "Sure, Abby. How nice of you to ask. Maybe some soda?"

Proud of doing the right thing, I grin. "No problem. See you tonight."

Resettling Hannah's ever-increasing weight on my hip, I walk the fifty-eight steps back home.

Barbara opens the door before I can knock, which is wonderful because I wasn't sure how to do it with a liter of 7-UP in one hand and Hannah propped on my hip.

"Abby, Hannah! So glad you could make it!" Barbara dresses for dinner, a foreign concept in my family. With her flowered summer dress and matching sandals, she looks like a sitcom mom. I've been to her dinners before, so I brushed Hannah's dark hair until it shone and put on my best jeans and a cami top.

"Barbara, you look fantastic." I kiss her cheek and hand over the 7-UP.

She ushers us through the entryway and into the dining room. Jackson, Cody, and Walt are already seated. We all greet each other, and I find it strangely difficult to look at Jackson. If he hadn't smoothed things over with Cody for me, we might never have had that incredible conversation in the car. So I'm grateful. But when I glance Jackson's way, it's not appreciation I feel.

Barbara serves a salad with walnuts and cranberries.

Beaucoup fancy. Hannah, locked down in a high chair, refuses to eat it. Barbara graciously fetches some saltine crackers for her. Jackson tells some funny stories from his trip. Walt asks Cody about school. Barbara inquires politely about Kait and Stephanie. It's all so civilized. I am totally loving it.

I help Barbara clear the salad plates and she brings in the main course, a strange-looking rice pilaf with mushrooms and asparagus. It's like one of those dishes you see on the covers of magazines in the checkout line at the grocery store. Hannah scrunches up her face so I run to the kitchen and find her a container of yogurt and some animal crackers to eat.

I am three bites into my pilaf when the phone rings. Walt pushes away from the table and answers the extension in the kitchen. "Hello," he says, and then there's a brief silence.

"Who the hell is this?" Walt's voice thunders in the room. We hear the phone crash against the floor, plastic against unforgiving tile.

Barbara's half out of her seat when Walt returns, intimidating eyebrows arrowed over his nose.

"Who was it?" she asks.

Walt waves a hand, speechless for a second. "They asked if my homo son was here. When I asked who it was, they said Cody's boyfriend."

My eyes shoot to Cody. He's pale. Barbara covers her mouth with a linen napkin, smothering her gasp. Jackson gets very busy shoveling salad into his mouth. Only Hannah seems unconcerned, happily dunking a cookie lion in her water glass.

"I don't have a boyfriend," Cody says after an awkwardly long moment.

"Of course not!" Walt shouts like he's still on the phone with the prank caller. "My sons aren't gay."

Two spots of color flame Cody's cheeks. He looks at me, swallows hard, and closes his eyes.

"Actually, Mom, Dad, I have something to tell you." His eyes open, wander the table before settling on Hannah.

"Yes?" Walt prompts, then stuffs a large spoonful of rice into his mouth.

"Mom, Dad," Cody starts over. He rubs his nose.

Jackson catches my eye like, *Is he about to do what I think he's gonna do?* And I shake my head like, *I have no idea.* Even though I have a bad feeling in my gut like I know exactly what he's going to do.

"I'm gay."

Barbara's fork clatters on the edge of her plate, then flips to the floor. Walt is frozen in place, color creeping up from his collared shirt, slowly inching its way up his face. So much for keeping it between us. It's one thing to field the harassment at school, but I guess a crank call at home was too much. Looks like Cody's coming all the way out. I give him an encouraging nod.

Hannah bangs her fist on the tray and sends a cookie elephant flying. "Wan' mine!" she screams, pointing at the floor.

Normally, if Hannah throws something on the floor, I leave it. Otherwise, she'll think it's a fun game and I'll spend every meal on my hands and knees tossing her food back up to her tray. This time, it is so awkward, and everyone is so silent, that I welcome the interruption. I slide out of my seat and grab the cookie.

Cody watches his parents the same way a small jackrabbit watches a coyote. "Mom, Dad?"

I am sick to my stomach, the pilaf like a brick in my belly. The longer they don't say anything, the worse it gets. Walt's face is now completely red, and I can actually count the heartbeats in his temple. One—two-three, One—two-three. His breath rasps loudly in and out.

Hannah munches happily on her cookies, fingers covered in yogurt and drool. She is the only one oblivious to the tension.

Maybe Cody planned this all along and the crank call just gave him an opening. Maybe he asked me to dinner tonight to make it easier. Maybe he is counting on me to do something. I take a deep breath.

"That's great, Cody!" I say too loudly.

Barbara sits, stunned, but Walt bellows out, "Great! You think this is great?"

I swallow. To be truthful, Walt has always made me a little nervous. As the branch manager of Valle Verde Bank, he works long hours. Outside of these Saturday dinners, where Barbara makes sure everyone is on their best behavior, I rarely see him. So I don't answer, just spear a forkful of asparagus and stuff it in my mouth.

Walt stands. His napkin slips to the floor. "Take it back, Cody. This isn't funny anymore."

Cody trembles in his chair. "I'm not being funny. You really think I'd make a joke about this?"

"I can't think why else you'd say something so outrageous." Walt thumps a hand on the table. Our water glasses rattle. Jackson's sloshes over and water seeps into the tablecloth.

Barbara rushes to Jackson with a cloth napkin, no doubt hoping to mop up the mess before it damages the wood table underneath. Jackson scoots to give her room to clean. Her hand shakes so badly that she knocks the water glass completely over.

"Damn it!" she shouts.

Cody and I both stare. We've never heard her swear. Never.

She turns on Cody. "Why do you have to ruin everything? Why?"

"He's not ruining anything," I say. "You knocked over the glass."

"Gay?" she repeats, clearly not having the same conversation I am. "I can't believe you'd tell us now. Isn't that kind of thing supposed to happen in college? Not *now*, for God's sake. Who will go to prom with you next year if you're *gay*?"

That prom is her primary concern here strikes me as funny. A giggle escapes. Four sets of shocked eyes focus on me. I wave my hand at my face, like a fan, but it doesn't stop the giggles. More erupt from me. "Prom?" I choke out. "You're worried about prom?" I can't stop laughing.

Barbara's chest heaves up and down like she'd just run her three-mile loop, and she takes a big gulp of water.

Jackson forces a chuckle, which pushes Walt over the edge.

"There is nothing funny about this!" he yells. The volume is so loud that Hannah looks up from sucking yogurt out from underneath her fingernails and lets out a yowl of her own. Once she gets started, it doesn't stop. She picks up volume and pitch until I worry neighborhood dogs will come running.

I pick Hannah up, yogurt-fingers and all, and jostle her on

my hip. "Shhh," I say to her, but look at Walt, hoping he'll take the hint.

He doesn't. "No son of mine is going to be gay. Get over this nonsense right now, Cody. You understand? Right now!"

Cody pushes his own chair back. He's unsteady, but mad. "This is exactly what I expected from you! I knew you wouldn't understand, I knew it!"

"Cody Matthew Jennings, watch your tone of voice!" Barbara returns to her seat. "Both of you sit down. We're going to finish this meal like civilized people." She goes for her fork, but when she can't find it, takes the spoon and cuts an asparagus spear in half.

I set Hannah back in her chair and retake my seat. Obediently, we all take a few bites of our food. The pilaf takes up too much space in my throat, and for a few tense seconds, I worry that I'll choke. Or suffocate. Or barf it back up onto my plate. I take a quick sip of water, and the rice finally goes down.

"So, Cody, how long have you known?" Jackson asks, either braver or dumber than I gave him credit for.

Cody finishes chewing, then answers. "For a while now, I guess."

Jackson nods like he's known all along, but I remember his reaction in the car. I feel strangely proud of him for being strong for Cody now. "Cool. Will you pass the salt?"

Walt springs from his chair again and shouts, "My son is not gay!"

"Of course not," Barbara agrees. "But we'll talk about this later when we've all calmed down."

Cody slams down his fork. "There's nothing to talk about. I'm gay. You know. End of discussion."

Barbara grinds her teeth, and I finally see where Cody picked up the habit. "I said we'll talk about it later."

"What else is there to say?" Cody says, making an obvious effort to appear emotionless. "I'm gay."

Walt starts to say something, but Jackson clears his throat.

"By the way," he says, "I'm not going to college next week."

Chapter ♥ 13

"What were you thinking?" I ask Jackson later. Hannah and I escaped the war zone shortly after Jackson tossed in his grenade.

It is hours later, almost midnight, and Hannah's down for the night. Jackson's convinced me to sit in the tree with him. We are squished up together, which was maybe his plan, and I'm leaning against him for balance.

When I look up, I can make out a few stars through the leaves of the trees. The night air is cool against my skin, a relief after the summer heat of August. It may crawl back up into the nineties again tomorrow, but while the sun's down, I actually feel like I should've brought a sweatshirt.

"I didn't see how they could get any angrier." Jackson shrugs off his timing. "I was wrong. They actually took his car back. Can you believe it?"

The Jennings family were amateurs when it came to family fights, but they'd been loud enough tonight that I'd closed Hannah's window so she could go to sleep.

"Sounds like it was World War Three," I say.

Jackson's forehead scrunches up. "I knew they wouldn't be happy with me. Why make Cody take all the parental rage when I had a share coming my way? It only seemed fair."

I lay my head on his shoulder, something I do all the time with Cody. But it feels different with Jackson. "How's Cody?"

"I don't think he's coming out of his room anytime soon."

Cody has hermitlike tendencies. It's not unusual for him to lick his wounds in private. I know he'll come out when he's ready. Still . . .

"Can you sneak me in tonight? I want to check up on him."

Jackson snorts. "Wish you were planning to sneak into *my* bedroom in the middle of the night."

I push against him, but not too hard since he's my balance. "If you're gonna start talking like that, I'm leafing."

He looks at me blandly.

"Get it? We're sitting in a tree? Leafing?"

He doesn't crack a smile, and I feel stupid. "Forget it."

Only then does he let a smile spread across his face. "Got you," he says.

"Jerk. You gonna let me in tonight or not?"

"Only if you promise to check on me, too." His face is innocent, but his eyes are teasing.

"Uh-huh," I agree. "Just close your baby blues and wait until I get there."

"I'm holding you to it," he says. "One good-night kiss in exchange for a sneak-in. Deal?"

"I didn't say anything about a kiss."

"What do you think's gonna happen if you visit me in my bedroom in the middle of the night? We're not playin' checkers, if that's what you're hoping."

"Maybe I won't stop by then."

"And leave Cody, your best friend in the whole world, all alone on what is possibly the worst night of his life? You can't do it, Abby. And you can't sneak in unless I turn off the alarm for you. So, deal? Right?"

I decide to negotiate terms once I'm inside their house. "Deal."

Jackson laughs and kisses the top of my head. "I'm suddenly feeling so tired. . . ." He swings one leg over the branch and onto the highest step.

"Wait." I stop him. He freezes in place, balanced on the old piece of wood, face turned up to me.

"Yeah?" His eyes are as dark as the sky above us.

"Do you think you're Stephanie's dad?"

He blinks once, very slowly. "Kait told me Steve's the father."

"But it could be you, right? If Stephanie wasn't a preemie, I mean."

He shrugs. "I'm not sure how. It was only a couple of times, and we used protection." He nods, and I'm not sure if he's reassuring himself or me.

"Condoms break," I say.

His face hardens. "Well, ours didn't. Kait says it's not me and I believe her."

I want to believe her, too, so I decide, at least for now, that that's enough.

"Good night, Abby." Jackson shimmies down the tree, leaving me alone on the lowest branch.

"Night, Jack-Off."

I watch until he is inside. He flips the lights twice, a signal Cody and I made up back in third grade, to let me know the alarm's disabled. I carefully pick my way down the tree and go into my own house, worrying because Cody has never given me rules about what to wear for breaking and entering. Guess I'll have to figure it out on my own. And I may as well brush my teeth, too, in case my negotiations aren't successful.

Homecoming. Your school probably has one, too, and there's a game and a dance and everyone talks about who's going with who. Maybe it's in the gym or maybe they rent a place. Wherever you have it, there are cheesy streamers and balloons and an even cheesier photographer who charges an outrageous amount of money for you to take pictures against his "fantasy" backdrop. It was the last thing I thought Cody'd want to talk about at one in the morning, but there you have it. He won't talk about dinner, about what was or wasn't said. How he's feeling or what comes next. It's all about homecoming.

"She's worried about prom, but come on, homecoming's less than a month away and who will I go with?" It's not like Cody to be overly dramatic. It's more like him to have already made a chart of all possible dating scenarios and ranked them in terms of cost vs. fun. I'm surprised he wasn't already at his laptop working on it. Instead, I'd found him half sitting in bed, lights out, brain revved up in high gear. Not even slightly amazed to find me creeping into his room so late, he'd been quick to scoot over and make room on his small bed. His only comment? "What took you so long?"

"You'll go with me," I say, answering his homecoming question. "Like we did last year. We had a good time, remember?" My voice is whisper quiet. Although Cody's parents are far down the hall and can sleep through anything, the darkness calls for soft words. Just like it also calls for black clothes, which is why my cat-thief outfit is black yoga pants and a matching tank top with little glittery butterflies across the top.

He sighs, very melodramatic, slides down in the bed, and draws the white sheet up to his chin. Although it's too dark to see it, he stares at the poster of the New York skyline tacked to his ceiling. "Don't you want your own date? The Plan will be under way by then, won't it? I'm not coming along to watch you suck face with some mediocre-looking guy."

Why that stung, I'm not sure. "Brian's better than mediocre."

"But he's not playing for your team."

"Doesn't mean we can't go as friends. We could all go as friends." Sounds like a perfect solution to me. Brian gets to go with Cody, Cody gets to pretend he's not gay, and I get to . . . be the third wheel. So it's not a perfect plan.

Cody reaches out from under the covers to hold my hand. I'm lying on my side, facing him, on top of the bedspread. Despite the warm cocoon, his hands are cool and dry. He laces our fingers together.

"Abby, you're the best. I'm sorry I've been so freaked lately."

"It's understandable. You're my Cody, and I love you just the way you are. I only want what's best for you."

He squeezes my hand. "That's what I wanted my parents to say. But I knew they wouldn't."

"Give them time," I say. "They'll come around."

"I'm not so sure."

"Relax." I stroke back his hair with the hand he's not holding. "The worst is over."

✦

It is not unusual in a soap opera for a femme fatale to sneak into a man's bedroom and wait for him on his bed. I've seen it on all of my soaps, but it's a particular favorite on *Moments of Our Lives.*

But this situation doesn't apply to me right now. Jackson is already in his bed, so I can't wait for him. Although I want to pretend to have forgotten our deal, I also don't want to be the one who backs out. Maybe Cody and I talked for so long that Jackson fell asleep.

No such luck.

"Right over here," Jackson says in a sleepy voice. "I'm all puckered up and ready."

I take one step into the room and close the door behind me. Jackson's room is even farther from their parents' than Cody's, but I'm not taking any chances. His room has the same basic layout as Cody's—bed, desk, shelves—but unlike Cody's room, always so neat and tidy, Jackson's looks like a tornado might actually improve things.

"About that deal . . ." I say.

"Nope, no backing out now. You made a promise and you're going to keep it."

He knows me too well. After having so many promises

broken in my life, I'd sworn never to do the same to anyone else. Of course, a deal isn't the same as a promise.

"Did you brush your teeth?" I ask to annoy him.

He laughs. "Did you?"

"No, and I've been sucking on a garlic clove all evening."

"I love garlic."

"And smoking."

He laughs so hard the bed shakes. "Abby, just come here. I'm not going to hurt you."

Gingerly, I pick through the dirty piles of clothes and discarded what-have-yous to the side of his bed. The outdoor light leaking in through the window illuminates a Barnes & Noble bag.

"You bought me a replacement Rumi?" I ask, toeing the bag open.

"I don't have to replace it. I never lost it."

"Then hand it over already."

"I told you I'm still reading it."

I reach a hand into the bag. "So what's in here?" I pull out a heavy book but can't quite make out the title in the dark.

"Mom's idea of a going-to-college gift."

"What is it?"

"A PDR."

"What, like an organizer or something?"

He laughs. "*Physician's Desk Reference.* Subtle, isn't she?"

I drop the book. It makes a muted thunk on the floor. "You could use it to prop open a door, maybe clonk an intruder on the head."

He pats the edge of the bed. "Stop stalling and get over here."

I sit. The bed smells like him, clean and fresh, his hair still damp from a shower.

"See, not so bad, right?" He's not even touching me. His face is shadowed, but what I can see looks dead serious. "How's Cody?"

"Okay, I guess. Considering. But you know him. He's not ready to talk too much."

Jackson sits up a little, and his white T-shirt stretches across his chest. He takes a deep breath, straining the fabric even more, and says, "I'm not sure what's going to happen. I'm just glad I'll be here for him, and not off at college."

"Are your parents raging about lost A.U. fees?"

Jackson is silent. "Come here." He gently pulls me toward him, rearranging my suddenly limp body so that I'm stretched out next to him. Like with Cody, he's underneath the covers and I'm on top. He rolls to the side and tucks my head under his chin, wraps an arm around my waist.

"Stay for a while," Jackson whispers. "I won't bug you about that kiss if you'll just lie here with me."

"Okay," says my mouth, which is so disconnected from my brain. My brain is saying that this cuddling thing could be a lot more dangerous to the Plan than a simple kiss.

He breathes out, tickling the hair at my temple.

"To answer your question, my parents are not happy with me," he says. "Really, spectacularly not happy."

"You did pick possibly the worst time to tell them."

"Hey, give me some credit. I was trying to draw fire."

"Were any ultimatums given? Any children disowned?"

His arm tightens around my waist. "They're putting my college money in a trust fund that I won't be able to touch until

I'm twenty-one. They think by then I'll be over my 'insane' desire to save the world."

"It's not insane." I sketch an invisible tattoo of my name on his bicep. "It's good. Kind of noble."

"You think?"

I relax back into him. "Yeah. I wish you'd tell me more about it."

He sighs into my hair and his fingers slide back and forth across my stomach. "It's kind of hard for me to talk about. Things are so different there. It was all so gritty and, I don't know, *real*. When you know there's a sick five-year-old who's going to die if you don't get the truck with the medical supplies back before nightfall, it makes you think about what's really important."

"Like what?" I calm his restless hands by trapping them at my waist. "What's important to you now?"

"I have to get back there." He drops his forehead to rest on my hair. "I promised Isabel I'd be back now."

I twist around to face him. "You have a girlfriend waiting for you?"

His teeth flash white in the dark. "Relax, Abs. She's eleven. She was teaching me Spanish."

"Oh." I flip back around and pull his arms around me again. "How'd you meet her?"

"She came to us—Carlos, he's the head of the relief camp, said she'd come before, when she was younger—and asked us to help find her big brother. She hadn't seen him in two months. He disappeared one night, and she's desperate to find him."

"How sad," I say, drawing figure eights between his knuckles with my finger.

"That's not the sad part. She'd been on her own since he disappeared, homeless. She was starving, sick, and one of her arms was broken when she came to us. She didn't even know it. Said it must've happened while she was sleeping."

My hands still. "How do you break your arm in your sleep?"

"You wanna know how an eleven-year-old homeless girl is treated? Like garbage. When people pass kids curled up, sleeping in doorways or in alleys, they kick them, spit on them. Isabel told me once a guy actually peed on her."

"So someone kicked her hard enough to break her arm and she didn't even wake up?"

"Isabel's used to it, but she told me how some kids she knows go to sleep in the Hotel of a Thousand Stars."

"That sounds nice," I say. "Pretty."

"It's a cemetery." His voice is flat, hard. "The kids sleep there because no one goes to graveyards at night. It's the only place they can sleep unmolested."

"That's horrible! All those children . . ." I think of Hannah, Stephanie, and the baby-to-be. "What about Isabel? Where is she now?"

"With Carlos, I think, but no one at the camp has time to help find her brother." He wraps himself more tightly around me. "That's why I've got to go back. So many people have let her down. I need to keep my promise."

I'm suddenly worried about him, going to this other country where things are so different, so horrible. Where a child can break her arm and lose a brother and nobody but Jackson cares. "Can't someone else look for him, like the police or something? It's not like you're the only person in the world who can help her."

His voice gets very soft. "There just aren't enough people, Abs. Not enough money. Not enough supplies. What I was doing there, it was *important*."

That's when I know he's going back, and probably sooner rather than later. He's following Rule #5, Get Out of Town, but he seems to not know the part about going somewhere romantic, like Hawaii—and, oh yeah, taking me with him.

"I hope you find her brother," is what I say.

Then it's quiet for a long time. His arm gradually loosens, and I think he's almost asleep when he says, "I wish I hadn't promised not to bug you about that kiss."

I roll so we are front to front. "Get over it."

But I don't get up and I don't leave. I tell myself Hannah's fine, tucked in my bed with Kait and Stephanie in the same room with her. No reason I can't stay for just a few more minutes, Jackson's arm draped over me, his chest rising and falling the same as mine. We fall asleep, breaths mingling, hearts beating their own distinct rhythms.

Considering I've always shared a room with Kait, and that Cody and I have had many a sleepover together, it shouldn't faze me to wake up next to Jackson. Sometime during the night, he'd rolled onto his back and the only way we are physically connected is that my calf is thrown over his knee. Even though I am still in my yoga pants, it somehow seems too intimate.

Jackson hadn't closed his blinds, and the morning light is bright enough that I think someone at my house might've noticed I'm missing. Or maybe Kait's just glad she doesn't have to worry about me walking in on her and Gustavo. Besides, it isn't the first time I've slept over at Cody's. So what's with the nervous fluttery feeling? The inability to move that stupid leg away from his knee?

"Oh, man," I say. "It's morning!"

"Don't worry," Jackson says, eyes still closed.

"Jailbait? Ring a bell?"

He cracks on eye open to glare at me. "Stop saying that."

"It's true."

"I don't want to fight about this. Nothing happened anyway." He overexaggerates a sigh. "Sadly. Tragically."

Looking up at him, I see the outline of stubble on his chin. I reach up and cup his jaw with my palm. Surprisingly soft. How much I want to kiss him grabs hold of me and won't let go. In the back of my head, though, I hear Shelby saying, *Have you noticed how much Stephanie looks like Jackson? It's remarkable, really.*

"Jackson?" I whisper.

"Yeah?" His lips are kissing-close.

"Are you sure you're not Stephanie's father?"

"God, Abby." He grabs my wrist and shoves my hand away from his face. "I told you things last night I've never said to *anyone*. And I thought you got it. Got *me*. But all you care about is something that happened six months before you and I ever got together? I've told you it's not me; Kait's told you it's not me."

We're still close, even though we're not touching. My leg

migrated back to my side during his talk. He's right. I know he's right. But . . .

"I just can't be with my niece's dad. You know how my family is. I can't be that girl. Like *them*." My stomach has gone from fluttery to tight. My throat is too thick to say any more. I've told him my biggest fear. He has to understand at least that much, right?

Jackson pushes himself into a sitting position and looms over me. "I'm tired of begging, Abby. I've told you over and over again what happened. Believe me or don't. I can't undo it, although I wish I could, and I can't be someone else for you."

"That's not what I'm saying. . . ."

"Just get out of here." He swings his legs over and shoves his feet into the worn flip-flops by the side of the bed. "I don't know what I was thinking last night."

I'm stung, but I struggle not to show it. That was supposed to be my line, you know, after the kiss. *I wasn't thinking. This was all a big mistake. It can never happen again.*

I pick my shoes up off the floor and slip them onto my feet. His bedroom faces the same direction as Cody's and has the same style window. Years of practice have me slipping out the window without a sound.

The Walk of Shame. Sneaking into your own home in the same clothes you wore the night before. Only nothing happened, but who in my family is going to believe a crazy story like that?

Chapter ♥ 14

No one ever bothers to lock our sliding-glass door. It glides open without a sound. I think my stealthy entrance is a success until I look up. My whole family, babies included, is staring at me.

There are a lot of families around here that would be at church at ten on a Sunday morning, but not mine. Kait, Stephanie, and Shelby, who apparently cut her weekend away short, sit on the sagging floral couch. Mom and the Guitar Player stand in the archway that leads to the kitchen. And most surprising, my dad's here, too, next to Shelby with Hannah on his lap. I attempt to tame my wild morning hair by trapping a piece behind my ear.

"Good morning!" I say brightly, wondering if they're all here because they thought I'd gone missing. "Lovely day for a walk, isn't it?"

"Abby! Thank God you're home!" Shelby breaks the silence in her usually flamboyant way, launching herself from the couch at me full speed. She swallows me up in a hug that leaves little room for breathing. I can't believe they are this worried about me. "I made Dean bring me back as soon as Dad called my cell this morning. You have to talk some sense into *him*."

Shelby points an accusing finger at the Guitar Player. I should've known the tears weren't for me.

"What's going on?" I ask, noticing for the first time how bad my dad looks. His eyes are bloodshot, and it appears that he's slept in his clothes. I see the faded plaid blanket and matching pillow on the couch. Make that slept in his clothes on our couch.

"Dad?"

"It's only for a few nights," he says. I begin to get the picture.

"But it's like, *man* . . ." The Guitar Player is clearly straining his brain in an effort to get a coherent sentence out. "You're divorced. You don't live here."

"I'm family," Dad says. "You have to put me up."

The Guitar Player wags his head and the light glints off the fake diamond studs, three in a row, in his ear. "Divorced, man. That means you can't be hanging around here, all in Mona's business."

Shelby bounces Hannah on her lap. "He's my dad and I say he can stay."

"Daddy stay, Daddy stay," Hannah chants in rhythm to the bounce.

Mom looks dazed, hands at her waist, standing in a direct beam of sun from the window. It's not a flattering light. There are tiny creases around her eyes, and without the full complement of makeup, her lips are dried and pale. The old sweats with the hole in the knee don't do anything to help the picture.

I sit next to Dad. "What happened? Shevon kicked you out?"

He swallows loudly and nods. "Just because I came home a bit tipsy, she said I have to sleep somewhere else. Like it's so easy to find a place to go at two in the morning. Then she said don't come back, she's changing the locks."

"But it's your house, right? You bought it." I give him an encouraging pat on the knee. "You can go back anytime you want. If Shevon wants to leave *you*, then she should be the one to *leave*. You with me?"

He's looking a little blank. "She said she's taking me to the cleaners. She's gonna get my house and my motorcycle and probably the fillings from my teeth if she can."

Motorcycle? I glance questioningly at Shelby. She shrugs like she doesn't know, either.

The Guitar Player stomps his booted foot. "He's not staying here and that's final."

I whip my head around to look at Mom. He may think they made up after the incident in the driveway, but long years with my mother have taught me that she can hold a grudge. Boy, can she hold a grudge. Her eyes get that sparkle that means someone's going down. Poor Guitar Player. He doesn't even see it coming.

"This is *my* house, and I will say who can and cannot live here." She whirls about and huffs off to the kitchen. Dishes clatter in the sink. She always cleans when she's angry. Too bad she's usually so easygoing.

Kait muffles a sob, hiking the baby sling up so she can bury her face in between Stephanie's head and shoulders. Her cries wake up Stephanie, and she joins in. I wonder if Kait has post-partum depression and then decide, yes, of course she does. She had her stepfather's baby. Who wouldn't get depressed? Brandi on *Passion's Promise* got postpartum after the birth of her baby, because Jake, the father, was married to someone else. But then Jake realized he was still in love with Brandi, and that cured her. I don't think Kait's problem can be so easily solved.

Someone's phone rings. Dad checks the clip on his belt but finds it empty. Kait shuffles through the diaper bag at her feet and produces her phone from one of the pockets with baby ducks marching across it in red raincoats.

"Gustavo! Thank God! Please, I'm begging you, come and get me. I can't live in this madhouse anymore!" She lurches to her feet and carries Stephanie, who is still crying, and the bag back to our room.

I can't say I disagree with her. "Really, Dad, do you think staying here is the best thing for everyone?"

"He's being selfish," the Guitar Player says. "This is what he always does. Comes crying back to Mona. *Oh, baby, please forgive me.* Well, she's not taking you back this time."

For the record, the Guitar Player is not entirely off base. This is exactly how Mom and Dad got back together after their first divorce.

Dad closes his eyes and then opens them again, clearly hoping this is all some kind of bad dream. "It's only a few nights. Until I find a new place."

"Get out!" The Guitar Player points to the door, very macho-like.

From the kitchen, Mom screeches, "He stays!"

Dad smirks. Not an attractive expression for him.

"You're not sleeping on my couch." The Guitar Player takes a threatening step forward. The couch is the only piece of furniture he brought with him when he moved in. Since our sofa was old when I was born, we were glad to see it go.

"It's not your decision." Dad stands, flinging the blanket behind him with a quick flick of his wrist. Dad and the Guitar Player are about the same height, and wear identical expressions of hate on their faces. I take a step back toward the sliding door, afraid of what I might be about to witness.

The doorbell rings and that's enough of a distraction to break the tension in the room. I hear Kait squeal, "Gustavo!"

He must've been nearby to arrive so quickly, although it's hard to imagine what could bring him out here besides Kait. Hiking, or maybe the Fry's by him ran out of his favorite brand of facial cleanser. After a few long, tense moments, Kait pulls Gustavo into the living room. "Mom, everybody, we have an announcement!"

Mom comes into the room, wiping her hands with a somewhat used dishtowel. "Yes?"

"Gustavo and I are moving in together!"

Shelby leaps to her feet, dislodging Hannah and making her cry. "No way. Not another one. Nine people cannot live here! It's impossible." She takes Hannah by the hand and whisks her away.

"Kait," I say, trying to be the voice of reason in this logic-impaired family, "isn't it kind of soon?"

Kait bounces Stephanie in the sling. "Are you kidding me? It's almost too late! Dr. Patty says that babies need the steadying influence of a father figure." She screws up her face like she's thinking real hard. "Otherwise, the child can develop attachment issues later in life," she apparently quotes.

I wouldn't call our father a steadying influence, which could explain a lot of things about me and my sisters. Maybe Kait's onto something with this book she's reading. Still, when I look at Gustavo of the skinny ponytail and giant zit on his chin, father figure are not the first two words that jump to mind.

"That's, um . . . great, Kait. But Shelby's right. It's a bit crowded around here lately." I gesture at Dad's discarded blanket as evidence.

She claps her hands together, as happy now as she was sad only a few minutes before. "You don't understand! He asked me to move in with him. At his place! Isn't it wonderful?"

Wonderful is not the adjective I would've used, but maybe I'm being harsh. In terms of the Rules, Kait's not doing so bad. Gustavo's not new, but he's a new kind of guy for her. Not heartbreakingly gorgeous, but not too bad, either, if he'd cut off that tail. As for the No Baggage rule, he seems too nice to have racked up psycho exes. And while they're not Getting Out of Town, he's at least taking her *across* town. All in all, I decide, not a bad start.

"Congratulations!" I'm the first one to say it, then everyone else chimes in. Shelby even offers to help Kait pack. Apparently, Kait can't get away fast enough because minutes later, they are down the hall throwing baby things into trash bags to take out to Gustavo's car.

Gustavo stands in our living room, huge smile on his face, Stephanie held high against his chest. If this is his lucky day, I hate to think what the rest of his life has been like.

"Welcome to the family," Dad says. "I'm Kait's father."

"Nice to meet you, sir," Gustavo says, extending his hand.

They shake and Dad says, "Now, you need anything, just let me know. I'll be staying here for a few days."

"You're not sleeping on my couch," the Guitar Player repeats. His couch is comfortable if a little saggy, but it's his. It sounds reasonable to me that he can decide who can and can't use it.

"He's staying," Mom insists.

"Not on my couch." The Guitar Player doesn't budge.

And just like that, I've got a new roommate. My dad.

It's hard to miss the six-foot-long HOMECOMING IS HERE banner hanging between two eucalyptus trees in the school's main quad. I hitch my worn-out green backpack from last year over one shoulder as Cody steers me toward the table under the banner. I let him, because I've never been so relieved to be at school in my whole life. Sunday dragged on, with Kait making umpteen trips for the move, and Dad taking up residence on her side of the room. I even woke up before my alarm clock— unheard of for me, especially on a Monday morning.

Now, Cody and I stroll toward the science building, crossing the busy square of grass like two geckos dodging their way across a city sidewalk, while I fill him in on the horrors of listening to my dad snore all night. Sawing logs doesn't even begin to cover it.

"Come on." Cody tugs me to a halt in front of the table with two student-council reps selling tickets. The eternally perky Becca Waters and her ultra-perfect boyfriend Kent Something are smiling matching too-bright smiles. I have never seen them apart. I have never seen them not smiling.

"Hey, Abby!" Becca calls. We—Becca-Kent and me—had Freshman English together last year, but this is the first time she's talked to me since then. "Don't you want to buy your tickets now?"

No, I do not. I lower my eyes and move forward, but Cody blocks me with a strategic elbow.

"We should buy our tickets early. At the door, they're almost twice as much."

I guess he listened to my pep talk after all, but I just wanted to show up at the dance all last-minute. Like, *Oh, the dance? We were supposed to buy tickets? Well, since it's so late anyway, couldn't you just let us in? Thank you so, so much Becca-Kent. You're the best!* Hey, it worked for the Spring Fling last year.

"Cash poor," I say. "Maybe next week." It's always better to ask for money after a payday.

"I got it. Two for you, two for me." Cody pulls out his wallet and a wad of cash. Then he buys six tickets.

"Six?" I question. "Your parents coming, too?" Hard to believe, but they'd once been Union Coyotes themselves.

Cody pockets the tickets without answering and walks ahead. I'm forced into a half-jog to catch up. He doesn't stop until we are in front of the admin building. Other students stream past us, the heavy double doors banging behind them.

"Look." He points to the giant bulletin board mounted on

the outside wall. It's inside a hanging glass case. The words MAKE OUR NEW STUDENTS WELCOME! march across the top of the board in cutout letters. Underneath are pictures of all the transfer students, with names and former hometowns typed underneath.

"Six tickets?" I say again. "That's hardly enough for all these people."

"Pick one," he says. "Any one."

I hold up my hand. "This is your idea of matchmaking? Choose someone off the new-student bulletin board?"

"Or you could ask a freshman." He tilts his head to indicate a trio of frosh boys coming our way, all lanky and freckly and much too short.

I laugh at this. "Yeah, right."

"There's nothing against freshmen in your Rules. Some of them are very tall."

"Everyone knows girls mature faster than boys. I'm not trading down."

"Urban myth. Besides, you're not trading anything. This would be a first-time purchase, yes?"

I ignore the last. "I'm pretty sure it's been scientifically proven. Girls are definitely more mature than boys. For example, I'm mature enough to know you don't pick a boyfriend out from a picture lineup."

"It says to make them feel welcome."

I shove him. "Seriously, Cody. Even if I chose someone to ask out, we don't need six tickets. What gives?"

"Two for you, two for me, two for Jackson."

Jackson? He must see the next question coming because he

adds, "Homecoming, remember? They actually send the alumni invitations to this thing."

And he needs two tickets because he's going to ask someone to go with him. Someone who's not me, thanks to the mutual-avoidance pact that's been in place since Sunday morning. My sisters are former Coyotes. I pray to God it's not one of them.

"What about you?" I say, not looking at the board and not asking who Jackson's taking. Because it doesn't matter, right? This is how I wanted it.

Two teachers come out of the building, balancing coffee mugs and stacks of papers. One is on her cell phone, which seems unfair since we're not allowed to have them in school.

"You gonna pick someone off this thing?" I ask.

A slow smile takes over his face. "Nope, I've already got a date."

"Oh my gosh!" I jump up and down. "Is it Brian?"

Scuffing his shoe on the pavement, he says, "No. I asked that freshman. The one I told you about."

"Hickey Girl? That freshman?" I'm stunned. Now that he's out, I thought things would change. Like he'd stop hiding the fact that he's gay.

"Actually, her name's Jenna."

"She's a girl," I needlessly point out.

"So? Doesn't mean we can't have a good time."

"Cody, what's going on?"

He shoots me a stubborn glare. "I'm taking my driver's-license test in three days. I want to drive. Is that so wrong?"

"No." Doesn't explain what Jenna has to do with this. I wait.

"Abby, it's not like I'm gonna find the perfect guy *here*. I told my parents I was confused, not gay."

It takes a moment for the words to penetrate my brain. "What? How could you?"

"We're talking about my *car*. My freedom. My chance to get out of here every once in a while. They said they'd take back the car if I didn't 'get my head on straight.' Now that I'm so close to driving, I can't live without that car."

"But you lied."

"Not really. I mean, it's not like I've ever been with a guy, so I'm not technically gay yet. Maybe I'm wrong. And if I'm right, well, I can always be gay in college."

"You'll be gay *in college*?" My voice raises. I hear an echo of my sisters' hysteria, so I tone it down. "How can you say that?"

"Why does this one thing have to define me? I'm a lot more than gay, you know that. But it's like once I say the g-word, that's all anyone sees. It's all so stupid." His jaw is set at the stubborn angle. The no-backing-down angle. "Besides, it's my decision. And I've decided that I don't want to be tormented for the next three years just because no one can see past the gay thing. You don't want me to be miserable, do you?"

New York is looking better and better. There, he could be who he is and not worry about what anyone else thought. "Okay, Cody. I get it. I want you to be happy."

He smiles and throws an arm over my shoulders. "So I decided to help you find your perfect guy."

"I can find my own guy," I say, although truthfully, I haven't been trying very hard. Or at all.

"Trust me," he says with a grin. He reaches into his navy backpack and pulls out his gigantic binder with all the tabs and color-coded labels. Opening it, he extracts two sheets of paper and hands them to me. "Here's everything I found out about the transfers." He gestures at the bulletin board. "You'll have to judge for yourself which ones are ugly enough to make your cut."

"Shut up." I smack his arm. "I'm not looking for ugly, just unremarkable."

"Same diff." He studies the pictures.

I look at his spreadsheet. A list of names runs down the side of the page. Boxes extend to the right. Rules #2, No Baggage from Past Relationships Allowed, and #5, Get Out of Town, are labeled across the top. Notations fill most of the boxes. "Has a cat," "Plans to be a marine," "College-bound," "Ex-girlfriend in CA."

"Wow," I say. "How'd you find all this out?"

"I have my ways." He smiles, proud. "So, who's it going to be?"

My eyes roam the bulletin board, scan the spreadsheet. But all I can think about is that Jackson has two tickets. Closing my eyes, I wave my finger over the bulletin board and point. "That one." I hope it's not a girl.

"Guess again," he says. "Here, I'll spin you."

I open my eyes. My finger is on Brian's picture. I think it's fate.

"One more time," Cody urges, but I shake my head.

"Nope." I tap the glass. "He's perfect."

Chapter ♥ 15

It's weird to even think it, but although it's only been one day since they moved out, I miss Kait and Stephanie. And not just because Kait took most of the clothes, including a few pieces that were mine, from the closet when she left.

I suppose if I wanted to, I could dip into Dad's side of the closet, do the cross-dressing, gender-blender thing. He has a couple of shirts and a suit neatly lined up on the far left. His jeans are folded over wooden hangers, and his polos and button-downs take up a foot of space. My clothes are on the right, and there's a great rift in between, a stretch of empty space between hangers that was never there before.

Stranger yet, there's men's shaving cream by the side of the bathroom sink and the toilet seat is up. I used to wish Kait was a brother, but now I miss her predictable bad moods. With Dad as a roommate, I can't quite relax.

Case in point. I walk into the room and he is on my bed reading. My bed. Even Kait, selfish roommate that she was, knew to stay on her side of the room. I am about to make some comment about personal space when I notice what he's reading. My journal.

More specifically, my very private poetry-filled, hidden-under-my-bed journal. Which means he's also found Mr. Manly, so I'm not so sure I should say anything.

He looks up and says, "Some of these are good."

A lie. I know my poetry pretty much sucks. That's why it's personal and private and hidden under my bed.

"That's mine." I snatch the book out of his hands. Then I don't know what to do with it. Or him. "How could you?"

"I'm not kidding. Have you shown those to someone, like an English teacher or something?" He actually looks proud, tucking his hands behind his head and beaming at me like I'm gifted.

"You had no right"—I shake the journal at him—"to read this. To go through my stuff."

"I know, I know." He sits up and plants his feet on the floor. "I was moving the furniture around, trying to make some room for my desk, when I found that box. I was worried it might be drugs."

"Drugs? Are you crazy?" My body trembles, like the beginning of an earthquake. I pace to the window and back. "How could you read my journal?" I knew I should've gotten one with a lock, but those had all been so pink and sixth-grade-looking.

"Sorry," he says, although he's clearly not. He leans forward, wrists on his knees, hands dangling in the air, and smiles at me like everything is made okay by an insincere apology. "But

about my desk? I think we can fit it there under the window."
He points to where Stephanie's crib used to be. Kait picked
it up on one of her many trips back to get stuff. It is the only
three feet of wall with no furniture pushed against it.

"No," I say, still pacing. I make a quick turn on my heel
whenever I get to the window, pivot again when I reach my
bed. Back and forth, back and forth, like a coyote waiting for
a deliciously plump pocket mouse to reemerge from its under-
ground burrow.

"Oh, it'll fit." He acts like measurements are the problem.

"No," I say again. "No desk."

"I need somewhere to work."

"You have a house."

He blows out a breath. "Shevon wants the house. You know
that."

"It's your house. Tell her leaving you means leaving. Period.
Put your foot down, for God's sake." I stomp my own foot to
help make the point.

"Don't take that tone with me, Abby." He folds his arms
across his chest. "I'm the parent here."

"Since when?" The earthquake inside me intensifies. I fling
my journal across the room. It hits the wall, spine breaking,
pages falling out in clumps. I can't take this, him, anymore. I
pull a Shelby, slamming the door behind me and then yelling
through it, "This is my room!"

I don't know where I'm going when I leave the house, but
fifty-eight steps aren't enough. I walk the neighborhood until
sweat plasters my T-shirt to my skin. When I get back, my

room is empty and Mr. Manly sits on my pillow. Whatever. I shove him back under the bed, rescue my journal, and carefully tape the pages back together.

"Abby, help me with this, will you?" Dad pushes a desk down the hallway. As he turns it into our room, it jams against the doorframe and sticks. He motions at me with his hand to grab one end of the desk, clearly forgetting our argument of just a few short hours ago and the fact that I'm completely pissed at him.

I don't get up from my bed. "It won't fit." It's not the desk from his house but some IKEA reject that's seen better days. "Where'd you get that thing?"

"Yard sale," he pants. "Down the street." He backs up and rams the doorframe again. A sliver of wood flies free.

"Take it back," I say. I'm scribbling out a new poem, one about asshole dads and their stupid-ass stupidness.

There's a loud thunk and a whole chunk of doorframe peels off.

"Damn it, Abby, get out here!"

"No!" I'm shouting now, even though I hate to sound like one of my sisters. "You will not bring that thing in here." I get up, cross the room, and slam the door shut.

"Abigail Savage, open the door right now!"

I get behind Kait's bed and shove it in front of the door. "No!"

There's silence on the other side. No yelling, no desk sliding on the wood floor. Then I hear a tentative tap on my door.

"Abby?" It's Mom. She would take his side.

"Forget it. The desk's not coming in."

"Abby, be reasonable. He needs a place to work."

"What work?" I grumble. It's not like hardware salesmen have briefcases to take home, clients to call, campaigns to prepare.

Mom's sigh is loud enough to penetrate the door. Cody can probably hear the disappointment all the way at his house. "He's starting his own business, Abby."

I respond with a sigh of my own. How many get-rich-quick schemes can one man have? This will end like all the others—in a fizzle of debt. Mom, though, never learns, and my silence catapults her into babble mode. "Imagine, a high-end store, selling kitchen and bathroom fixtures for all those new developments going up everywhere. Isn't that a great idea?"

She takes my continued silent treatment as agreement and continues. "There's a lot of research to do, things to organize. He needs some space."

"How about his house? There's plenty of room to work there." It's true, too. He and Shevon had a house bigger than ours. Why he has to mooch off us, I don't understand.

"Abby."

"Mom." Her heels click down the hallway. I press my ear to the door and hear Mom say, "Give her a little time, Carl. Maybe in a day or two, she'll be more reasonable." The desk scratches away.

I watch from my window as Mom and Dad half-carry, half-shove the thing down the driveway. I've won, but I wonder at what price?

✳ ✳ ✳ ✳ ✳

I have to say one thing for Dad. There's better quality beer when he's around. He's not shy about using it to buy forgiveness, either. He hasn't come out and said it, but I can tell from the fact that he bought imported beer instead of domestic that he realizes our earlier fight was his fault. I'm feeling mellow, like maybe I was slightly overreactive about the desk and maybe he wasn't as horrible as I recall. Lucky for him, writing non-rhyming poetry in erratic meter always makes it easier for the amnesia to set in.

"This Steve guy, he's all right?" Dad asks. We sit in the kitchen, each nursing a Heineken. Everyone else is in bed, so it's unnaturally quiet. The *tick-tock* of the clock over the archway punctuates each second as it passes. The fork and spoon hands point to the different vegetables. We started at broccoli—eleven—and now the spoon has passed carrot—twelve—and is heading toward the green pea that is one o'clock.

I shrug because I don't like to talk about the Guitar Player. Not that anyone in this house has ever asked for my opinion about him before.

"I'm worried about your mother." His hand clenches and unclenches the can so that his words are punctuated with an irritating crackle. "She's had some bad times, y'know? I want to be there for her."

"You're divorced," I remind him. "And still married to Shevon."

"Your mom's a hard woman to get over." His mouth droops, and I think he's trying to squeeze a tear out.

"Don't hurt yourself," I say. "No need to cry in your beer for my benefit."

"But he treats her right?" He gets that tear out and lets it run down to his chin.

"I don't know." My beer is no longer cold, so I slug the rest back before it gets any warmer. "I guess so."

What I really think is that the Guitar Player is a total schmuck and a loser, but if I say that, Dad might decide he has to do something about it, and frankly, just having him in my room is all the tension I can stand. I may have won the battle of the desk, but he's still living here.

"How'd they meet again?" Dad thoughtfully gets us both another beer while continuing the Guitar Player Quiz.

"He subbed at our school one day. Kait found out he played guitar and arranged to take lessons from him. They dated for about a month, until she brought him over and he met Shelby."

"Shelby looks just like your mom," Dad says. "Beautiful women are hard to resist. Used to getting whatever they want, too."

I continue my story. "He dumps Kait for Shelby. Kait announces she's pregnant with his child. He takes off for a few weeks then comes back 'to do the right thing.' But Mom was here that day, and he took one look at her and decided the 'right thing' was for him to give Kait money for an abortion."

"It can happen like that. One look's all it took for your mom and me."

The fact that my mom flings herself from one love-at-first-sight relationship to another is no news flash. The fact that Dad is not outraged by the Guitar Player's callous treatment of his daughters is also unsurprising.

What is surprising is when Dad says, "Good for Kait for turning down the money."

I laugh. "She took the money and used it to buy baby clothes. He was furious. I think that's why he was out of town the weekend Stephanie was born." And also so he could screw around on my mom, but I don't say that part.

"This new guy Kait's with, this Gustavo. You like him?" Dad has a row of three finished beers in front of him. He pops open a fourth. I'm still on number two.

"Well enough. I don't think she would've moved in with him so soon, though, if you hadn't . . ." It's rude to tell your dad he pushed his child out of the house, but I see he gets my message.

"I thought they were in love," he says.

"One of them is." Gustavo had it bad, as far as I could tell. I wasn't as clear how Kait felt. Relieved to be out of here, probably. Shouldn't you move in with someone because you love them? Not just because your family drives you crazy and you think your baby needs a dad?

Dad leans forward and rests his head against his forearms. This is his resting-between-drinks pose. I toss my cans in the trash and head back to my room. Our room. And I can't help wishing Kait and Stephanie would move back in and Dad and the Guitar Player would move out.

Chapter 16

"Look, Abby, I really don't think you should ask Brian to homecoming." Cody is too lazy to walk over. He's harassing me over the phone. Apparently, an entire day at school has worn him out. I'm tired, too. After only a few hours of sleep last night, classes seemed to drag on forever. And I'm not so sure the Heinekens with my dad helped too much with the weekly Tuesday quiz in Computers today, either.

"It's not like you're going to ask him." I am trying to get the last bit of stubborn nail polish off my big toe. I'm so over purple nails.

Dad opens the door without knocking. Why should he? He lives here. He sighs loudly, kicks off his shoes, and sits on the edge of Kait's bed. His bed. I can tell he wants to talk.

"Cody, it's a done deal. I just got off the phone with him, like, three minutes ago." I am lying. Cody probably knows it.

"You know what you are, Abby? A coward."

"I'd be careful with words like that. Have you looked in the mirror lately?" I toss the used cotton ball toward the trash. It hits the rim and lands on the floor. Dad stares pointedly at it. I flop backwards on my bed and look at my ceiling. Right above me is a series of cracks that has always reminded me of a crushed skull. I find it comforting.

"Abby? Hello? Don't make me come over there." Cody's voice is agitated.

"There's no room for any more people in this house." This time I glare pointedly at my dad. A private moment to talk on the phone would be appreciated.

"Abby, we need to talk," Dad says.

I hold up the one-minute finger. "Cody, leave it, okay? You picked Jenna and the universe chose Brian for me."

"I'm not so sure it was the universe," he says. "You must've been peeking. Twelve other male transfers on that board and you happen to pick him? I'm not buying it."

"He fits the Rules," I say, wondering if Cody will dare bring up that Brian is gay. Then I will point out that the Rules say absolutely nothing about being gay. I roll onto my side and switch the phone to my other ear.

"Oh, he's got baggage, all right," Cody warns. "Face it, Abby. You only like him because you think he's safe."

My eyes narrow, which is useless since he's not here to get the nonverbal message. "Brian's a nice guy."

"A safe guy."

"What's wrong with wanting to feel safe? To have someone in your life who isn't going to possibly impregnate one of your sisters? Is that too much to ask?" I squash a pillow under my head with such force that the other pillow, the one that usually ends up on the floor by the end of the night, bounces in place.

"He doesn't like you like that," Cody says.

Interesting. "How would you know?"

Cody is silent. I hear his slow exhale of breath. "We've been talking."

"Oh, really. Isn't that fascinating? What could the two of you possibly have to say to each other?" The crushed skull smiles down on me.

"We talk about speech class," he answers too quickly. "What else?"

Dad points at his watch, like that is supposed to mean something to me. Still, it's not like I want to talk with him listening to every word so I say, "Gotta go. Maybe I'll come over later and we'll continue this intriguing conversation."

We hang up. When I look over, Dad is standing.

"That was rude," he says.

"Wasn't it? I mean, blatantly eavesdropping on someone's private phone calls? What are you? The government?"

He doesn't get ruffled. "I don't have much time and I needed to speak with you."

I am slightly alarmed by his formal tone. "What's up?"

"Your mom and I have been talking." He sits back down and loosens his salesman tie. "About you girls."

Since they are our parents, this shouldn't be shocking news. "And?" I prompt.

"Shevon's getting her own place. I'll be moving back to my house in a few weeks and . . ."

"A few weeks? What happened to a few days?"

"Abby, focus here. What I'm saying is that we've decided when I go, you should move in with me. I've got another bedroom. You'll have it all to yourself."

Flabbergasted. I am completely speechless.

"I've seen how tight it is here, how hard this situation is for your mom. I just want to do what's right."

Since when? He takes over my room, rifles through my stuff, tries to bring in a desk like he's a permanent resident, and now he's taking off, back to his old house, old life, and the right thing is for me to go with him?

"No." It's the only word I can think of. "No, no, no."

"You'll like it," he goes on like I haven't spoken. "You'd have your own bathroom."

Now that is some bait. Imagine a bathroom where I don't have to worry that someone else has used my towel to wipe places on their body I don't want to think about. A bathroom where no one uses the last of my conditioner and then refills the bottle with water. I am so tempted by this vision of paradise.

"You'll still be able to go to Union and see Cody there every day."

Not live next door to Cody? How shallow am I that I'm willing to desert him for unlimited hot water and hair accessories that stay where I leave them?

"I have a better idea," I say. "Why don't you actually make your child-support payments so Mom doesn't have to worry about money so much? In fact, why don't you offer to pay a little more? I'm going to need some cash for a homecoming dress."

"Abby!" he says in this shocked voice. "I have always paid your mother child support."

Yeah, when the court ordered him to. When he didn't need

it for something else, like his honeymoon to Hawaii with Shev-on or the down payment on his house. When Mom paid extra money, which she didn't have, to get a lawyer to file complaints against him. Like I said, you can't count on this guy.

"Forget it," I say. "I'm not moving out. Just pay Mom what you owe her."

He rubs his forehead. "I can't believe you don't want to live with me. Think of it, Abby. Your own room. Maybe even a car?"

"A car?" I ask, because Cody would understand that kind of temptation. And with a car, I could always be at his place and it would be like I never moved out.

Dad clears his throat. "Well, eventually. We'd have to see how it goes."

Even an eventual car is better than the no car I'm getting now. I'm not saying it isn't tempting, but who will take care of Hannah when everyone else is working? Who will make sure Shelby doesn't siphon gas out of Mom's car and sell it to her friends for cash? I have to live here. They need me.

A concept my dad clearly doesn't get. "Are you sure? You're always complaining about how crowded this place is."

"That doesn't mean I want to move out."

"Kait did."

"Well, I didn't just possibly give birth to my stepfather's child, so I'm not in as big a hurry to relocate." Kait sure had been, though. I hadn't heard a word from her since she took off with Gustavo. Mom says they talked on the phone and she and Stephanie were fine, but I guess I'll have to go to Blockbuster if I want to see my sister again. I wonder if she's checked in with her alterna-teacher yet and if she turned in that *Bell Jar* essay. It took me forever to type that thing into Cody's computer. It better have gotten an A.

"If you're sure," Dad says, interrupting my thoughts and looking more than a little relieved. That's when I realize he's trying to make amends. He actually made a grand gesture for me, and although he was scared I might say yes, he did it anyway. I almost choke up. Almost.

I decide there are other ways he could make things up to me. "I really could use some money for homecoming. I need to pay Cody back for my tickets and get a dress."

"Can't you wear one of your sister's dresses?" This is the one thing my parents always agree on. Why buy Abby something new when we can just give her a dress that's years out of date?

There should be some benefit to spending so much time with my usually absent father. I give him my most pitiful look. "Please, Dad."

He breaks down and reaches for his wallet. "Okay, Abs. Will this do?"

He holds up a few bills. It's not as much as I would've liked, but better than wearing Shelby's hand-me-downs.

I shoot across the room, from my bed to where he sits on his, taking the cash and hugging him in one smooth move. "Thanks!"

He pats my back. "Glad I could help, pumpkin. I want to see you in that dress, you hear?"

"We'll take lots of pictures."

"Well, now that's settled. I'll tell your mom what we decided."

I step away. We didn't decide anything. My eyebrows crunch together. "What?"

"I'll stay on here until Shevon moves out. Maybe Shelby and Hannah will want that room in my house."

Why does he insist on ripping our family apart time after time after time? Sure, Shelby's a pain in the butt, but what chance will Hannah have in life if the only people raising her are Shelby and Dad? This is so like my father, never thinking beyond the moment. Like Rule #4 says, Don't Need Him. Because you'll always be let down.

Two hours later, Cody and I are in our tree with a bag of Cheetos and a six-pack of Diet Cokes. This is our comfort ritual, and we are both in grave need of comfort.

"Dad's not buying it," Cody tells me. "He keeps popping into my room unannounced. Like he expects to find me doing something gay."

"Like what?"

"Wild monkey sex with male models? I don't know." He stuffs five Cheetos in his mouth and crunches down.

"But you told him about Jenna. What more could he want?"

"Maybe I have to sign some kind of declaration. I, Cody Jennings, in order to form a more perfect family, establish my straightness, insure Jennings family domestic tranquillity, provide future generations of Jenningses, do ordain that I am a card-carrying heterosexual."

I crack up. "Thomas Jefferson would die if he heard you mangle the Constitution like that."

"What's it to him? He didn't even write the thing. But he was kind of a control freak, so I guess it's good he's already dead. I'd hate to give one of the founding fathers a coronary." Two swigs of Diet Coke, two Cheetos. "Not that he was in any position to judge others. I'm doing this paper on him and, man, did he have some issues."

I snake my hand in the bag and grab some Cheetos for myself. "But about your issues, Cody. What're you going to do?"

"My driver's-license test is in two days. If I pass and he hands over the keys to my car, then I'll know I'm in the clear. If not, I don't know what I'll do."

"Tell him he's right?"

"Abby, we're talking about my car! Imagine, driving and driving until we're out of Cottonwood, out of Arizona, heading east toward the Big Apple. I thought you were with me on this?"

"You said we didn't have enough money yet." I lick Cheeto dust from my fingers, then dive in the bag for more.

Cody crushes the soda can and drops it to the ground. It lands with a thunk against the others we've been piling up for the last hour. "We don't have nearly enough cash, but getting the car's all part of the master plan, right? We need jobs and we can't get jobs unless we have wheels. So I've got to do everything I can to convince my dad that I'm straight, straight, straight."

"Aside from dating girls, which you are already doing, what else can you do? Either he believes you or he doesn't," I point out.

"Maybe we could have sex in front of him and then he'd know for sure which team I'm on." He winks at me.

"Gross!" I cannot for one second think of having sex with Cody. "You know I'm saving myself. But maybe one of my sisters . . ."

He laughs. "If only life was as easy as your sisters."

I wiggle my back against the bark of the tree for a good scratch and suck more cheese dust off my thumb. Cody is not a finger licker. Orange fingerprints decorate his new Diet Coke.

"You gonna tell me why you're scarfing Cheetos like they're about to be put on the endangered list?" Cody asks. "Or do I have to guess?"

So I tell him about my father and the desk and Shelby and Hannah maybe moving out and before I know it, I'm crying. "Why's he such a jerk? Why?"

Cody puts an arm around my shoulder, a tricky maneuver up here in the tree. He rubs his chin on the top of my head.

"I don't know. It's not fair. You're such a great person. It's hard to believe you came out of that house."

"Hey, you know I'm the only one allowed to rag on my family."

"I know." His chin bumps up and down on my head as he talks. "I'm just saying not to take it so personally. It's not your fault he is who he is."

"What if I turn out like them? Any of them? The Rules are working so far, but what if they're not enough?"

Cody knows this is my biggest fear. He knows it's why I have the Rules. In his usual way, Cody takes a long time to answer.

"Here's the thing, Abs. I don't think the Rules are good for you."

"What? They're working great."

"If by *great* you mean keeping you from having any kind of romantic relationship, then yeah, they're great."

I squirm away from him, but he hauls me back against his side.

"The one thing your family's good at is taking risks. You know, they just put themselves out there with no thought for the consequences. In a weird way, it's kind of cool. They're fearless."

"They're humiliating," I say. "You know better than anyone what a mess my family is."

"I'm not saying you should be like them, but I don't think the Rules are keeping you from turning out like them. I think they're keeping you from being. Period."

"Shut up."

"No, Abs, you need to hear me. Love is risky. The Rules don't allow for that. Maybe you shouldn't ask Brian to home-coming. Maybe you should take a risk, ask someone you really want to be with."

Like Jackson, who's been avoiding me since the night I stayed with him. Outside of the rides to and from school, chaperoned by Cody, we haven't seen each other at all. Which is how I wanted it, but somehow I can't get those two homecoming tickets out of my mind. One for him and one for *someone else*. Not that I've asked or anything, but who needs to? One plus one always equals two.

"Brian and I are all set," I say. "I told you I already asked him."

"A perfect example of how the Rules aren't working. You're

going to the dance with a gay guy. How's that going to get you closer to True Love?"

"It's not getting me further away." I know he's right. I stuff more Cheetos in my mouth.

Cody gets intense, puts a hand on my cheek, and forces me to look at him. Into him. "Abigail Elizabeth Savage," he says, laying on the seriousness, "relationships are messy. People screw up. They hurt you. But when you love someone, you forgive them. That's what a relationship is, Abby. Good times and bad. Together."

I bite my lip and nod.

"Promise you'll think about it. The dance is only a few weeks away. Anything could happen between now and then."

"Thank you," I say.

He smiles and takes a swig of Diet Coke. "Enough heavy stuff. Let's talk about something else."

"How about what I'm going to wear to this dance? If you pass your test Thursday, will you drive me to the mall? Dad gave me some money for a dress."

He squeezes my shoulder. "Of course. Why do you think I want my license so much? It's only so I can chauffeur you around, cater to your every whim, especially on *my* birthday."

"Cody!" I slap his arm, but not very hard. "You know you're dying to pick out my dress. What better present could I give you than total control over my wardrobe?"

"It's true I probably won't get much else, since my parents already gave me the Camry. Dinner and a cake is all I've got goin' on that day." He's grinning, though, because the car is the only thing he wanted anyway.

I flip my hair, Shelby-style. "Sweet-sixteen shopping, then? You'll find me a dress that doesn't make me look like a wanna-be bride?"

He looks at me with a critical eye. "You know I'm going to say red."

"You know that's Shelby's color."

"Blue?"

"Kait." That's the problem with too many older sisters. There's nothing new for me.

Cody claps his hands together. "Don't worry, I'm going to find you the perfect dress!"

I swallow my last Cheeto of the night. "Finally, some good news! What're you thinking?"

"Let's go to my room later," he says. "We can go online and check out the latest Betsey Johnson collection."

I crinkle the empty Cheetos bag into a ball. "I can't afford her."

"Come on, dream big. Maybe we'll find something great on sale." Cody leans forward a bit and stares at me in his *I dare you* way. "You feel like making a deal?"

"Sure, you can borrow my eyeliner for homecoming."

"Hey!" he tosses one of the cans at me. "Be nice or I'll dress you like a bridesmaid."

Ducking, I catch the Diet Coke with one hand. "What then?"

"I've got something to show you." He reaches into his back pocket, all mysterious.

I'm intrigued. What could he possibly have tucked away that would save me from bridal-party-close-out-sale fashion?

Chapter 17

The spreadsheet is something of a letdown, although I'm not sure exactly what I'd been expecting. That he'd already bought the perfect dress, folded it into a pocket-sized square, and then sat on it for hours before revealing it?

"You showed me this already, remember?" I finger the edge of the heavy card stock. It's the same breakdown of transfer students, attributes listed column by column, abbreviated so they'll fit in the boxes.

"Yeah, but now I've assigned a value to each of the Rules. If you go by the last box, you can start with the guy with the highest score and work your way down." Cody looks exceptionally pleased with himself.

I check out column six. It's unclear to me how the system works, but everyone has a score somewhere between one and ten. It seems kind of, well, heartless.

"You're scary sometimes, you know that?" I give the list back to Cody. "I can find my own boyfriend."

"Really? Exactly how many dates have you been on since you came up with the Rules?" He's acting pretty sure of himself, which is understandable. Because we both know the number is zero.

"Shut up. I just haven't found anyone yet."

"Be honest. Have you even been looking?"

Of course not. I'd been so busy not looking at Jackson that I didn't have time to find anyone new with no baggage who was average-looking and wanted to run away with me. I keep thinking of Saturday night at Jackson's and how it'd been so great until I'd opened my big mouth. The only person possibly more disgusted by my behavior is Jackson himself, which makes our forced carpooling that much more awkward. Because as much as I want to throw myself at him, as much as I understand what he said about the thing with Kait being in the past, I can't pretend like Stephanie might not be his daughter.

"Let's do this thing," I say, handing him the list. "You choose one for me. I don't care who. I'll call him when I get home and ask him out."

"Really? An actual date-date?"

"Yep, maybe a movie or something."

"Then let's go with Mr. Ten." He points to the first name. Andre Castillo. Perfect score in box six. His phone number is in column two.

"But let's not wait," Cody says, and places his cell phone in my palm.

I dial.

Jackson's horn honks outside my window and I wince. Why had I stayed up so late on a school night, two nights in a row?

Wednesday, usually my favorite school day because it means Bio Lab, is already off to a bad start.

"Mom!" I screech down the hallway. "I'm gonna be late!"

More barfing sounds. We need a bigger house if for no other reason than to give Mom morning-sickness privacy. "Sorry!" she calls. "I'm trying to hurry."

Now I feel bad. It's not her fault the baby makes her puke up her breakfast. I just hope this phase passes as quickly as it came. "Don't worry," I say. "I'll brush my teeth at school."

My toothbrush comes skidding down the hallway in response. Nice. Thanks, Mom. But I guess the dirt'll wash off. I pick it up and stuff it in my backpack.

"Abby?" Mom's voice is unsteady, as is her whole body where she props it against the bathroom doorframe. She holds out a tube of toothpaste to me. "Can you do me a favor?"

Jackson honks again.

"Sure." I take the Crest and stuff it in next to the toothbrush. "What do you need?"

She sways and it looks like she might heave again. Then she swallows hard and says, "Can you call the agency for me? Tell them I'll be late. Again."

"No prob," I say, since this has pretty much been my job all week. "Angie and Bob said yesterday that they hope you feel better soon and not to worry about coming in late. Angie's got your back."

Mom smiles, but it doesn't erase the gray tinge from her skin or the dark bags that have taken up permanent residence under her light-blue eyes. "Thanks, Abby. You're a wonder."

I am? It's so unusual for her to outright compliment me—

unless it's to note how I look like her—that I'm momentarily stunned. Man, those pregnancy hormones can totally whack you. "I'm glad someone finally noticed," I say, and she laughs.

I almost tell her that Angie's planning a baby shower, but although it's still a few months away, I decide Mom's probably not in much of a party mood right now. It seems unfair that a baby you can only tell is there if you look really hard can cause such havoc. I wave, and Mom closes the bathroom door. When I slip into the backseat of Jackson's car, Cody hands over his cell phone without my even having to ask.

"Was Kait this sick?" Cody asks when I've relayed Mom's message to Angie and assured her that no, Mom has no idea about the shower and yes, I can keep it a secret until January.

"Nope, not at all," I say. It was lucky for her since she hid her pregnancy until the second trimester.

We ride along in silence until Jackson turns on the radio, loud. It's some news show, so we listen to reports of traffic for places where we aren't, until at last, he pulls into the school drop-off zone. Cody hops out first.

"Abby," Jackson says after turning down the radio. "Wait a sec."

"What?" Since *that* night, he hasn't initiated a conversation with me.

He gives me an envelope. "This is for you."

Well, obviously. It has my name in his sloppy handwriting on the outside. I start to break it open, but he says, "No, for later."

So I get out of the car, but as soon as the Corolla's out of sight, I rip open the letter.

Rumi. He copied one of my favorite passages, about how love delights even in distance and disagreement.

It's unfair to use Rumi against me. I can't stop thinking about the words, what he might mean by giving them to me. What does he want? It doesn't matter, I tell myself. I have a date with Andre on Saturday, and no Rumi-quoting possible father of my niece is going to get in the way of my One True Love Plan finally going into effect.

Cody and I eat lunch outside whenever we can. The weather's generally accommodating, so we have a favorite spot under one of the many cottonwood trees that line the greenway behind the cafeteria. We sit on the half wall that separates the grass from the sidewalk and balance our lunch trays on our laps. I shove Jackson's note at Cody before he even has a chance to take a bite of grilled cheese.

"My brother?" Cody asks when he's done reading. "Jackson's actually quoting poetry?"

"It's not fair, is it? He used to be a stupid jock." I reread the note for about the thousandth time today.

"And it's your favorite poet." Cody sneaks a bite of sandwich.

"I *know*."

A couple guys, baseball hats turned backwards, pass by and take seats a few feet down the wall from us. A brown-and-white woodpecker hammers away at our tree.

Cody chews. Sips his apple juice. "What do you want me to say?"

My grip tightens on the edges of my tray. "Tell me what to do."

"Don't you have a date with Andre this weekend?"

I nod.

"Do that."

Hmm, that's not what I wanted Cody to say. That poem is seriously messing with my head. Maybe I don't have time to wait for True Love. Maybe I need to apply Rule #5 to myself and Get Out of Town before I screw up my life just like my sisters did.

"Cody." I set my tray aside and lean my head against his arm. "We could still go to New York. Do you want to go? Now?"

"My driver's-license test is tomorrow. I'm not going anywhere until then." He finishes off his sandwich and moves on to the container of fries.

"Silly, I don't mean right this minute." I pat his thigh. "We could go Friday."

"We've only got enough money to get as far as Illinois. Do you really want to end up there?" He levers a fry into my mouth and says in the self-helpy way that Kait quotes Dr. Patty, "Abby, I think we have to figure stuff out here, or else nothing will be different when we finally do get out of this place."

"Did you get that off your tea bag this morning?" I ask. Barbara buys those herbal teas with the inspirational sayings dangling off the end of every string.

He reddens. "I told you, Brian and I have been talking. Think about it, Abby. How will running away make things better?"

I have a list all ready for him. "No one will know my family. I won't have to worry that guys are only into me because they think I'll put out like my sisters. I won't have to share a room with my own father." I could go on, but he stops me.

"Okay, you have some points. But what about your Rules? I thought you were so set on making them work."

"Won't they work in New York?"

Cody drops his tray to the ground and slides an arm around my waist. "New York with no money would be a disaster. Let's stick to our plans, Abby. We just have to be patient."

Too bad I really suck at being patient, but I rest against Cody and let him convince me that things are looking up.

Chapter ♥ 18

Cody's not going to find the perfect dress for me. He's sixteen, licensed to drive for three whole hours now, and clearly longs for his own line of prostitutes to command.

"Too slutty," I say for what must be the tenth time. Does he not understand that just because I *have* it doesn't mean I want to *show* it? At this rate, we'll spend the remaining two weeks before homecoming right here at the Nordstrom outlet store.

"How will you know unless you try it on?" He shoves an armload of dresses at me, pastels and primaries, tulle and sparkles, all mixed together.

"If it needs a special bra, I'm not wearing it." I peel off the first two dresses from the pile—both strapless—and a gown from the middle that has only one strap and hand them back.

Cody shoves some blond hair out of his eyes. "You're being difficult."

"It's homecoming, not a Dress to Get Laid Party." I discard another dress from the pile. Too . . . pink. Then I wander away, toward the back and the signs proclaiming a BIG SALE is under way. Toward other like-minded shoppers, picking their way through the 70 percent off rack. Maybe I should try choosing something for myself. I hold a black dress with a flowy skirt in front of me. Not bad.

"It's homecoming, not a funeral." He yanks the dress out of my hands. "Did we or did we not agree that I'm to have total control today? It's not much of a birthday present if you're going to argue with me about every little thing."

"Fine," I say. "But I'm trying this one on, too." I snatch back the black dress. "If I buy this one, we can pocket the extra money for the New York Fund. Isn't that worth considering?"

Cody closes his eyes like he's in pain. "I'm telling you, *that* is hideous. Don't you remember the First Day Freshman Year Debacle? I warned you against fuchsia, but would you listen?"

Even worse, pictures of me in that hideous outfit littered the yearbook. I'd been so in love with it, I wore it every other week. If only I'd seen how big it made my hips, how small my chest!

"But this is black," I say half-heartedly, knowing I've lost. "Isn't black slimming?"

"You don't need slimming!" he all but shouts, then runs a hand through his hair and calms down. "Now come here. You're trying on the strapless green one and that's an order."

I shuffle along behind him. Isn't shopping supposed to be fun? Besides, we have almost two whole weeks until the dance. It's not like this is an emergency. Cody picks gowns off racks as we pass them until he has a new armful. He leads me to a changing room, hangs the dresses on the one hook, and says, "I want to see them all."

Huffing out a breath, I slide the heavy burgundy drape across the opening and shimmy out of my tank top. I'm struggling to zip up an aqua-sparkly number—why are zippers on the back?—when I hear voices outside my curtain.

"What do you think, Kent? I don't look fat, do I?"

I peak my head out, and there's Becca Waters, turning circles in front of the three-panel mirror outside the changing rooms. Her gown is pink—unrelentingly pink—with a full skirt and cap sleeves. Kind of like a princess dress, if you're seven years old.

"You look great," Kent says, his eyes on her cleavage where it peaks out above the scalloped neckline.

Becca turns and tries to see her back in the mirror. There is a huge pink bow right over her butt.

"It's not too much?" she asks, straining her neck for the rear view.

Kent stands and walks to her. He puts his hands on her hips and their eyes meet in the mirror. "You look beautiful," he says.

Cody's snort is so loud, I worry he will accidentally let some brain fly.

Becca spins. "What? Is something wrong?" She pats down the bow in the back.

"Something?" Cody echoes. "No, something's not wrong."

"Oh, good. I just love this color." Becca smiles at him.

Cody looks like he has just tasted something foul and can't decide whether to swallow it or hurl it back up.

"It's not that *some*thing's wrong with that . . ." Cody seems at a loss for words, then recovers. ". . . monstrosity. Everything's wrong. The color is horrible, that bow makes your butt look three sizes bigger. And Becca, really, cap sleeves with your upper arms?"

Becca's eyes fill with tears.

"Hey, man," Kent says. "That's not cool."

"Are you saying I'm f-f-fat?" Becca's tears brim over. "I j-just lost five pounds, you know. It's not like I'm not trying!"

"Oh, God," Cody groans, finally coming out of fashion-nazi mode. "That's not what I meant at all."

I step out of my room, still half unzipped. "Cody, go find her something good." I shoo him back to the racks and go to Becca's side.

"Will you zip me?" I ask her. She gulps back tears and yanks up the zipper. My breasts are squished against the unforgiving fabric.

I turn in a circle, even though there's no way I'm wearing a dress that makes me feel like a stuffed sausage. "What do you think?"

Becca blinks. "It's nice," she says hesitantly.

"Aha!" I say. "You're one of those. A changing-room liar."

She looks confused. Kent comes to her side and holds her hand.

"Don't lie to me. I'm about to pop out of this thing." I take a deep breath and the zipper actually slips down about half an inch. "See? And when Cody comes back, he'll point out how it looks like I've got a roll of fat right here." I point to the spot above the tight waistline where there is a slight bulge. "But it's not me—it's the dress. So I'll keep trying on whatever he picks out until we find the one, the *perfect* one. And then he'll make me get some uncomfortable shoes and tell me how to do my hair. That's just his way. He's got strong opinions."

"I guess," Becca says. "But I really liked this dress."

"Well, you can't wear it now, can you?" I turn so she can unzip me. "You'll keep thinking about what Cody said and you'll feel terrible. I think that's why he's like that. If he's nice about it, you might buy the dress anyway."

"Stop talking about me," Cody complains. He hands me two more dresses and then gives Becca a selection of five to choose from. None of them are pink.

"I like pink," she says.

Cody visibly tamps down his response. "Pink is too obvious for you. With your coloring, all that blonde hair, those gorgeous blue eyes, you can do something sophisticated. Hollywood glamorous, instead of so, so . . . Barbie."

Kent laughs and Becca whacks him on the arm. "Okay," she says. "I'll give it a try." She disappears behind the burgundy curtain, and Kent takes his place back at the boyfriend bench. She's on dress four when we hear a squeal from her changing room.

"Becca, you okay in there?" Kent asks.

"Look!" Becca emerges, no longer a high-school sophomore with chunky arms but a 1940s movie star about to walk the red carpet. The dress is a deep blue that pools around her feet with an elegant swish as she walks. The neckline plunges sharply, drawing the eye down, with a cinched waist that shaves off ten pounds. "I love it!"

"Obviously," Cody says. He walks around her and approves

the low-cut back. "Amazing. Now, let's talk hair. It's the details that are gonna make or break this look."

A discussion of up-dos follows, along with Cody's advice about jewelry: "Keep it simple. That dress is all the decoration you need."

Becca admires herself in the mirrors while I try on another dress that turns out to be as chest-flattening at the last one. I'm feeling a little jealous of Becca and her super fashion find, so I'm relieved when she changes back into her jeans and pink peasant blouse.

"Thank you, Cody," Becca says after hearing a mini-lecture about where and how to find the perfect shoes. "I never would've picked that color blue for myself, but it's absolutely perfect."

Cody grins at her. "It was fun."

"Yeah," she says with a giggle. "See you tomorrow."

With a wave, she and Kent are gone. Me, I'm still in changing-room hell.

"Maybe I am getting fat," I say from inside my cubicle. I twist around, contorting myself so I can get the zipper at least partway up my back. "All these things are tight."

"It's called *fashion*," he says. "Get out here and I'll help."

I push back the curtain and do a little twirl for Cody. He finishes zipping me and stands me in front of the mirror.

He smiles. "I'm a genius. That's the one."

One look in the mirror and I know he's right. "You *are* a genius!" I give him a quick hug, partially for finding such a great gown and partially out of joy that I don't have to try on anything else.

Back in the changing room, I slip it off and look at the price tag. "Cody, it's on sale!"

"This is a perfect birthday!" he jokes. "Hurry up, will you? I'm ready for smoothies."

I bundle up my things and head for the line at the cash register. After I pay, we zigzag through the aisles toward the exit.

"What about your present? You ready for that?" I ask, dodging a middle-aged woman looking at formal dresses by herself. What's that about?

I can tell Cody's pleased, but he says, "Abs, I thought we agreed the best present we could give each other was to put money in the New York Fund."

"It's just a small thing." I'm about to reach into my canvas tote and give it to him when a big guy cuts in front of us and blocks our way.

"Should've known we'd find you here."

"Hey, Craig," I say, clutching the plastic hanging bag in my suddenly sweaty hands.

Cody shrinks a little when he sees that Sean is also here.

Before they can start, I say, "What're you boys doing in the Juniors Formal section? Planning something spectacular for homecoming?"

For reasons I don't understand, Craig and Sean have always steered clear of me. Not that I'm complaining. I just wish the invisibility shield covered Cody, too. They act like I haven't spoken.

Sean picks up a glittery red dress off the closest rack and tosses it to Cody. "Your color, Cody?"

"Not really." Cody catches the garment in one hand. His

fingers fidget with the hanger. The dress dances.

"Be serious, Sean," Craig says, his bushy brows bouncing up and down with his words. "We all know Cody wants something a little . . . faggier." He grabs the pink dress Becca'd been talked out of. "Your boyfriend would like this, wouldn't he?" He laughs.

"I don't have a boyfriend." Cody clenches the hanger. The plastic snaps.

"For your information," I say, "Cody's going to homecoming with Jenna. Jenna Harris? A girl?" I am all for Cody being gay. I am not interested in seeing him humiliated in public.

"That fag hag?" Sean snorts. "And it's not hard to wonder why you've never had a boyfriend, Savage. I've heard gays all stick together."

I don't think, just grab something off the nearest rack and throw it. The hanger beans Sean on his temple.

"Bitch!" He rubs the spot. "You'll pay for that."

"Yeah?" I advance toward him. Dresses drop off the racks as I pass, arms swinging. I grab another empty hanger. "Bring it on."

The saleswoman who rang up my dress is suddenly by my side. "Can I help you with something?"

"I've got this under control," I tell her. I have the new hanger raised in perfect throwing position.

She gently takes it from my hand. "Perhaps I should call security?"

"No," Cody says at the same time I say, "Good idea!"

"Come on, Sean," Craig says. "They're not worth it."

"Losers," Sean calls out before joining Craig in a hasty

retreat. They take a right at the entrance to the store, toward the food court and Kactus Kal's all-you-can-eat buffet. Neither one looks like he's ever missed a meal.

"Wusses," I say to Cody. "I can't believe they're even considered human."

Cody doesn't look mad. He stares blankly at the scarlet dress still in his hand.

"Hey." I snap my fingers. "You okay?"

"They'll never leave me alone," he whispers. "It doesn't matter what I do. Who I am. There's no escape."

I've seen Cody like this before. The only cure is intensive retail therapy.

"Can we focus on what's important here?" I tug him out of there and in the direction of his favorite shoe store, DSW.

"That they're Neanderthals and when we live in New York, we'll never have to talk to guys like that again?" Cody's trying to play it cool, but his face is pale.

"True." I agree. "But more important, ta-da!" I reach into my tote and whip out a tiny box wrapped in sparkly paper.

"What is it?" Cody rips open the gift and pulls out a dark-green Matchbox car.

"I know you really wanted a convertible," I say. "Notice how I spared no expense? It's a Jag."

Cody laughs so hard he actually doubles over. "Abs, oh God. It's too perfect. Thank you!"

I laugh with him and sing a whole round of "Happy Birthday to you!" as off-key as possible. Heads turn our way, but I ignore them. We walk through the mall, hands linked, and the best part is that Cody can't stop smiling.

Chapter 19

Andre Castillo is black. Not that it's a bad thing, it's just there aren't so many black people in Cottonwood, so you'd think I'd have noticed him before. Cody was right. I hadn't been looking very hard.

"Whatever you want. I'm not picky," Andre says as we browse the movie posters outside the theater. He was surprisingly accommodating when I called out of the blue and asked him out. Now I'm finding that *accommodating* is possibly the very definition of Andre Castillo.

It's Saturday afternoon and there are lots of people around, couples holding hands and gaggles of middle-schoolers hanging in big clumps. We cruise the row of ads slowly while a dad with two sons tries to talk them into skipping the movie and just going for ice cream. He's not having a lot of luck, and it looks like the little one's getting ready to pitch a major fit. Dad sees it, too, because he breaks down and buys tickets for yet another one of those animated penguin movies.

"This one?" I point out a poster with teenage ballerinas against a snowy background.

Andre doesn't even blink. "Sure. Looks good."

Not picky is an understatement. "How about this one?" I ask, indicating the newest Jet Li action movie. "His stuff is usually good."

"You saw *Fearless*?" Andre's expression finally changes, looks interested.

"And *Hero*. Three times." Cody loves Jet Li movies. Finally some payoff for watching all those fight scenes. "He's really amazing."

"Yeah." Andre buys our tickets and our popcorn. He holds doors open for me.

Andre Castillo is the perfect date. No wonder he scored high on Cody's rate-o-meter. Andre's new, and judging from our short conversation thus far, has no scary baggage attached. He misses his home in Southern California, so he's also a good candidate for Get Out of Town. And he's not dog food in the looks department, either. Still, as he gestures to the third row of the movie theater and asks if I want to sit there, I don't feel anything. Not excited or put off. Not fluttery in the tummy, not upset. Neutral. It feels like we're going through the motions.

The previews start. We munch our popcorn. Andre says something to me and I nod. I'm not what you'd call focused on this date. And it's all Jackson's fault. The few times I've seen him—the last two chauffeur trips before Cody got his license—he acted the same. Like we were still avoiding each other. And I guess we are, because he hasn't called or come by and I sure haven't sought him out. I just read the Rumi poem over and over again, even though I've basically got the whole thing memorized.

The poem runs through my mind like a song you can't get out of your head. I can't stop thinking about the words, what he might mean by giving them to me. I let Andre hold my hand as my head replays the words Jackson chose.

Eventually the movie I've barely been watching rolls its credits and Andre says in his very nice, pleasant voice, "Want to go next door for a coffee?"

We sit at the Starbucks sipping our matching caramel espressos. We talk about school, teachers we have in common. He drives me home. We say good night. He kisses me and all I can think is: *He's perfect. For someone else.*

"Night," I tell him, pushing on his chest so he'll back up. No need for a second kiss: the Web poll is in, and the fans definitely want him off this soap, my own personal *Disasters of My Life.*

"I'll call you?" he says.

"Sure." Because it's not his fault he doesn't know me— how I think and what thrills me. "We could see that penguin movie."

He laughs. "Whatever you want."

What I want is not the point of the Rules, which is why I change my mind and kiss him one more time. I want his perfect score to be enough. But it's not.

A week passes. I see Andre at school and he's friendly enough, but he doesn't call. So he felt it, too, or rather, didn't feel it. No sizzle. Cody says I should ask out the next guy on the list and he's probably right. But I don't. I'm losing faith in the Rules.

Jackson's gone. Cody says it's because their dad kept

threatening to "haul his ass to college whether you like it or not," so Jackson took off to stay with some friends in Phoenix. I don't ask for details like, when will he be back? Because it doesn't matter. Shelby's visited Kait's new place and says Stephanie looks more and more like him every day. Jackson is definitely off the menu.

School drags on. Nothing explodes in Bio Lab, a big disappointment for me, but I don't give up hope. Homecoming Fever infects everyone so that all you hear in the halls are conversations about who's going and not going. Will we win the game? And, of course, what're you wearing?

Brian eats lunch with us under the cottonwood tree more often than not, and Becca-Kent always wave when they see us around. At home, Dad and the Guitar Player have reached a kind of truce, and Mom's morning sickness has eased up. Things are smooth and drama-free, exactly how I always wanted my life to be. I couldn't hate it more.

Chapter ♥ 20

I am a princess. Or at least someone who is very, very rich. That's how I feel, decked out in the dress Cody found. It is strapless and snug on the top, its cool gray color spilling out in layers below the waist. When I move, the fabric shimmers with hints of blue. It makes my eyes look mysterious. It makes me feel like someone else. Best of all? Built-in bra! This dress has turned tonight from a dull school dance into an *event*. Cody's right. Details *do* matter.

Cody rings our doorbell. His dad permanently forked over the keys two weeks ago and hasn't taken them back, so all is well in Operation I'll Be Gay in College. When I open the door, he stares.

"What?" I flip a piece of hair over my shoulder. Shelby helped me flatiron my layers into submission. She also did my makeup, smoky and dark. I can see my eyelashes when I blink.

"You look"—his eyes dart down and check out the strappy heels that glitter beneath the hem—"incredible."

"Thanks! You look fantastic, too." He seems taller in his dark suit with the muted green shirt. "Now come in. Mom and Shelby want to videotape us."

He groans but comes along anyway. "I've already been through this at my house. And I won't ever forget your leaving me to face that all alone."

"We'll have plenty of pictures together since we'll be doing this again at Brian's and what's-her-name's. Admit it, this hair was worth the wait."

"Jenna." He ignores my hair and shoots me an annoyed look. "I know you know her name."

"Smile!" I say in response. We pose for the camera, make some faces.

My mom grins from behind the camcorder. "You both look so grown up. I can hardly believe it. Oh, I wish Steve was here to see you." She tears up, which I know must be the hormones. The Guitar Player is all of ten miles away, playing happy hour at the Rockin' Rodeo. She doesn't seem to notice that Dad isn't here, either, but he'd told me he had a dinner with Shevon tonight. God, how I hope she takes him back!

Shelby comes over and fusses with my hair. "Stop touching it!" she says. "You're ruining the shape."

Excuse me for breathing, I think, but don't say it. After all, Shelby did find Hannah a playdate so she could help me primp. Imagine trying to keep Hannah's fingers off this shimmery dress.

I twirl around to show how my dress swirls at my feet. Cody grabs me around the waist, and we do an awkward box step on the kitchen linoleum.

"Show's over," he announces, looking at the clock. "We don't want to be late."

Some people are coming to the dance from the game. Cody and I decided to skip the sports part of homecoming because, as he said, "Who cares?" But I know Jackson's at the game, because I saw him take off in his Corolla hours ago. Cody said Jackson wasn't home two hours this morning before their dad laid into him about the whole college thing. *Poor guy,* I think, but then remind myself that I'm *not* thinking about him.

"Ready?" Cody holds out his arm, and I place my hand on his elbow, like you see in movies. We stroll out to his car and he even opens the door for me. Very fancy.

I have a moment of panic when we get to Jenna's and I see her outfit, a much shorter and more casual dress. It's black with a narrow white band under her breasts and makes her look model-thin. Her caramel-colored hair hangs to her shoulders, curly and wild, and she's wearing flats. Cody seems to read my mind, because he reaches over and puts a warm hand on my bare shoulder. "Relax, there's room for both of you in a semi-formal dress code."

We go through the photo shoot with Jenna's mom, who is a shorter, plumper version of her daughter with a wide smile and the smallest digital camera I've ever seen. She poses us in front of the staircase in the entryway. Boughs of greenery wind through the railing. When I accidentally brush up against them, they poke me with their fake, plastic needles. Silk flowers, a bit dusty on the petals, decorate a small table on the side with a plate full of keys.

"Just the girls," she says, arranging us with sweeps of her hand so that Cody stands to the side and Jenna and I are facing the camera with matching forced smiles.

"Sorry," she whispers out of the side of her over-glossed lips. "She's not usually like this."

I shrug one shoulder. "Don't worry about it. My mom cried."

"How about one with Cody in the middle?" Jenna's mom interrupts our brief moment of bonding. We arrange ourselves to her specifications. "And how about just the happy couple now?"

Jenna fits herself to Cody's side for the last shot, gazing up at him with what can only be called puppy-dog eyes. Cody sends me an SOS look, but this is all his idea, so I let him hang. "Take a few more," I say to Jenna's mom. "Can you e-mail me copies?"

Cody's teeth grind, but he stays put until Jenna's mom has taken approximately one gazillion pictures and gotten my e-mail address. And then, finally, we're on our way again.

At Brian's house, he meets us out front. His dark hair is gelled into submission.

"For you." Brian presents me with a small wrist corsage.

"It's beautiful," I say, admiring the way the tiny lavender orchids go perfectly with my dress.

"Cody told me what you'd be wearing. Orchids mean beauty and refinement."

I actually blush. Me. Cody laughs and touches a finger to my hot cheek. "Ouch!" he says, shaking it like he's been burned.

Jenna doesn't laugh. Instead, she looks peeved that Cody didn't bring her a corsage. I know he blew his budget on his black-and-white wingtip oxfords. And no dance was worth dipping into the New York Fund.

Brian's dad, who is older than any of our parents and sports a full shock of white hair, takes more pictures. We stand in front of the juniper tree in his front yard. Now that Brian's involved, we have the All of Us Together, the Boys Only, the Girls Only, the Separate Couples, and the Waving Good-Bye, Get Us Out of Here Pose. Just when we thought we could leave, Brian's mom drives up at the last second and we have to go through it all again.

"Thanks!" she says, brushing long strands of hair as dark as Brian's away from her face. "I didn't want to miss such a big night. I'm so glad you've made friends here. And it looks like you've even met someone special." She looks meaningfully at me, and I immediately see that she's in denial with a capital *D*.

"We're just friends," I say, about to push hair behind my ear until I hear Shelby's voice in my head saying, *Don't touch it!*

"Of course, of course." She slips her camera into her purse. "I'm glad I got to meet you, that's all I mean. Traffic from Tempe was impossible. I thought I'd miss the whole thing."

"I would've sent pictures, but I'm glad you made it." Brian, who is at least a half foot taller than his mom, leans down and kisses her cheek. "Are you going to stick around?"

She laughs. "Would you believe I have to rush back for your brother's game? I promised him I'd be there by halftime. Hope the traffic going the other way is better." She hops back in her little Honda and drives away without ever saying a word to Brian's dad.

"Interesting," I mutter to Brian in a low voice.

He flashes me a quick smile and shakes his head. "That story's too long for tonight."

"Another time?" I ask.

"Let's not borrow trouble," he says, and offers me his elbow. Since I practiced with Cody, I know just where to put my hand. He leads me to the car, where Cody and Jenna are waiting, and finally, we're off.

Although most of our school dances are held on campus, for this occasion, the student council rented space at the American Legion Hall. Cody drops us off in front, then circles around to park. We enter the building with Brian playing the role of a ladies' man, one girl on each arm.

"Hi, Abby! Got your tickets handy?" Becca, decked out in all the Hollywood glamour Cody chose for her, holds out one perfectly pink–manicured hand. A gold bracelet with tiny charms tinkles. Cody will definitely have something to say about that. I distinctly remember him telling her to keep it simple.

Brian hands over our tickets, all four, and explains that Cody's on his way in. Ever-present Kent tucks the tickets in a metal box. Kent's tie matches Becca's fingernail polish. Cody will have something to say about that, too. Kent smiles and says, "Have fun!"

"Decorating was such a challenge," Becca explains when we don't move along fast enough. "You wouldn't believe the restrictions. No tape, nothing can hang from the walls. It was a nightmare!"

"Honey, it turned out great." Kent lays a soothing hand on her back. "You were brilliant."

She dimples up and he leans in for a slow kiss. With tongue. We make our escape.

The main decorations are balloons. There must be a million of them, in every color. Each table has a balloon centerpiece and confetti scattered over it. I'll give Becca "colorful," but "brilliant"? No way. We settle at a table close to the dance floor and put down our stuff. Most of the tables are empty, but a few have been staked out by early birds like us. No one is dancing to the nineties grunge rock the DJ's playing. Understandably.

Cody was right about the dress code. I see two girls in jeans over by the buffet table, and behind them, three girls in what could easily be wedding gowns if they were white. They survey the food on the table and amble away without getting a plate. Must be the usual dance fare—stale sugar cookies and room-temperature cheese with unsalted crackers. Yum. Lucas Fielding, who's hanging out with a couple of guys I don't know, sees me from across the room and waves. I nod in his direction and lean back in the folding chair.

"Drinks?" Brian asks, and Jenna and I both say yes.

After he leaves, Jenna and I watch each other. The DJ has the music cranked so it's hard to hear her when she asks, "How long have you known Cody?"

"Forever," I shout back over the thrumming bass of house music. "You?"

"We met the first day of school." I think she blushes, but it's hard to tell in the dim lighting. It makes me mad, what Cody's doing to her. He knows he's not ever going to kiss her again, and here she is blushing over him. I never thought Cody would be one of *those* guys.

Brian comes back with three tiny plastic cups filled with something red. It looks like it has lethal staining potential, so I pass. Brian bobs his head to the music. Jenna keeps checking the door for Cody. It is taking him a long time, considering how few people are in the hall. Maybe he's not good at parking yet and drove out to the edge of the lot so he'd be less likely to hit someone's car. That seems right.

Jenna's face lights up. I turn my head and see Cody come in the door. He has a tightly leashed quality—like something's about to blow and only the strength of his will is keeping it in— that lets me know whatever the problem was, it wasn't parking.

"Cody!" Jenna meets him halfway and hangs on to his arm. "Wanna dance?"

Cody shakes his head no, causing a few bangs to fall loose from the tight hold of his hair products. His eyes bore into mine. He jerks his head in the direction of the bathroom.

"Excuse us," I say, taking him away from Jenna and apologizing to Brian with a look. "We'll be back in a sec."

Jenna pouts but brightens up when Brian rises from his chair and asks her to dance. The DJ has thankfully moved into this century and is playing some classic Beyoncé. Jenna bounces out to the dance floor, Brian a few steps behind.

We pass a few groups of people dancing and hurry past the photographer with his cheesy balloon arch. It looks like most of the people here are in the photographer's line.

"What is it?" I ask when we are finally in the hallway with the bathrooms. The music is still loud, but at least now we don't have to shout. "What happened?"

He pulls something out of his pocket and shoves it at me. It looks like a plug of some kind, only too skinny to be useful on any drain I've ever seen.

His face flames. "I can't believe this."

I turn the plug over. It's cool and smooth in my hand. "What is it?"

"It's 'for"—he waves a hand behind him—"like if you're clubbing and you plan to . . . hook up . . . this is to get"—he waves behind him again—"you ready."

"Huh?"

Cody is the worst person to have on your team for anything like Pictionary or Charades. He does the same useless gesture again and says, "You know, you put it in . . . "

I really thought after years of watching my sisters screw up their lives, I couldn't be shocked. But I am. Because what he's telling me is that it's some kind of butt plug. *Butt plug*. I drop the thing on the floor and back away from it. God, I hope it was new.

"How do *you* know about these things?" It's not like Cottonwood has so many happenin' clubs, or any for that matter, that this kind of stuff would be common knowledge.

Cody looks at the floor. "I, y'know, read stuff."

"Read stuff?" I can't take my eye off the *plug*. Try to picture Cody using it and can't.

He kicks the plug aside with the side of his shoe. "Web sites, chats—y'know, the usual."

I had no idea the usual could be so unusual. I mostly surf the Net for soap-opera gossip in Computers whenever Mr. Edwards isn't hovering over our spreadsheet assignments.

"Where'd you get these"—I can't say the words *butt plug*

aloud—"things?" I ask. He may have read about them, but he wouldn't bring them to homecoming. If they were his, he wouldn't be upset.

Cody's shoulders shake, but it's not fear this time. I think he might actually be mad. "When I walked in, someone pelted me with a handful of these things." He pulls another one out of his pocket.

"Who?"

"I don't know. I grabbed a few and came to get you. Abby, what should I do?"

Now I see that he is scared, too. Mad and scared and trembling like it's twenty below in here. A guy in a light-gray shirt brushes by us in the hallway, still zipping up his pants. Why do guys leave the bathroom before they're completely done? I mean, really, no one wants to think about what else you forgot to do while you were in there. The deep bass of the music rumbles the floor beneath our feet.

"We're telling the chaperones," I say. "That's what they're here for, right?"

"No, I mean what do I *do*?"

"We have to tell someone. This has to stop."

"Abby." He falls back against the wall, making room for two girls with matching clutch bags to get by. "I was really looking forward to tonight. Jenna's a nice person. Why doesn't it matter that I came with her? I mean, I could see before, when I never dated, that people could think I'm gay. But I'm here with a *girl*. How can they do this when I'm here with a *girl*?"

"I'm a girl," I say. "If being seen with a girl was all it took, you wouldn't need Jenna."

He waves his hand in a hopeless gesture. "But everyone knows you and I never . . . I mean, Jenna's like a real girl. Not a friend girl."

"Oh, Cody." I wrap my arms around him. He is too upset for me to get upset about not being a "real girl." I don't worry about my makeup as I smash my face against his coat. "I'm so sorry."

"What do I *do*?" he repeats into my hair. "I don't know what to do."

I, too, am at a loss. I don't know what to tell him. I don't know what to say. But it occurs to me that there is someone here who might. I detach myself from Cody and go get Brian.

Chapter ♥ 21

"What's going on?" Jenna asks. Cody and Brian have now been gone for almost an hour. She's had five glasses of the red punch, and it's stained her lips a berry color. She nibbles on her second stale sugar cookie.

"Guy stuff," I tell her, giving her the same answer every time she asks. Which is, like, every five minutes.

Finally, the guys emerge from the dark hallway and join us at the table.

"You okay?" I ask Cody, even though the music is so loud I'm not sure he can hear me across the table. But he nods, eyes red and chin set in stubborn mode. Whatever Brian said moved him from sad to mad. Cody watches the dancers, not so many that the floor is crowded, as they jump up and down to some hip-hop song I've never heard before. All of the guys have lost their jackets, if they even started out with one, and there's a pile of heels in front of the DJ.

Without a word to anyone, Cody stands and makes his way through the dancers to the DJ. He yells something, and the DJ leans closer. They shout back and forth, then Cody returns. When he sits, he pulls his chair closer to Brian and whispers something in his ear.

"What's going on?" Jenna asks again.

"Guy stuff," I say, since Cody doesn't answer her. His eyes are glued to the DJ, his hand on the back of Brian's chair.

There's a loud shout at the entrance. The football players arrive as a group, pushing through the door. They are loud and happy, so I guess they won. Lots of people rush them, slapping backs and laughing. For the next twenty minutes, more and more people stream into the dance. Cody never takes his eyes off the DJ.

The DJ takes the mike and says, "This one's for Cody."

Jenna screams and claps her hands as the DJ slows things down with Fergie's "Finally." If this were a soap, Cody and Brian would rise and gallantly offer us their arms. The edges of the screen would go blurry as if we were in a dream. The song would play and we'd swirl in each other's arms. Brian would dip me. I'd laugh.

But instead, only Cody stands. He holds out his hand to Brian, who takes it. They walk to the middle of the dance floor. The DJ shines a light on them.

"What's going on?" Jenna asks, looking panicked.

"Guy stuff," I say, smiling. "Wanna dance?" I hold out my hand. Because in the few seconds it's taken all this to happen, the dance floor has cleared. Only Cody and Brian are on the cheap wood floor, arms around each other, swaying to the music.

The edge of the dance floor is crowded with spectators. I hate the way Cody's shoulders are hunched, how he hides his face in Brian's shoulder.

"Come on," I urge Jenna. "We can't leave them out there alone."

She shakes her head, hand over her mouth. "Oh my God!" she says, and runs for the bathroom.

Someone whistles at Cody and Brian, that hot-girl-walking by-a-construction-site whistle, and some other guys join in.

"Fags, go home!" someone else yells, and I think I recognize Craig's voice. I tense, ready to pounce on the next person who says anything.

Instead, I feel a big hand land on my shoulder. "Can I have this dance?"

Angling my head up, I see it's Jackson. He's smiling at me but looks as tense as I feel. There's a leftover smudge of yellow face paint—one of the Coyote colors—under his left eye that matches the tiny yellow stripes in his button-down shirt.

"Thank you," I say, and he leads me onto the dance floor. We pick a spot close to Cody and Brian. I loop my arms over Jackson's big shoulders, and he spans my waist with his hands.

I force my shoulders to relax, move my feet to the slow beat, and listen to the words of the song. Of course Cody would pick this one. He's always loved it.

"Did you know he was going to do this?" Jackson's breath is hot in my ear.

"He brought a girl." I have to stretch my neck to look up at him. "He wants that car so much. I can't believe he's doing this now."

"Me, either," Jackson says. "Getting a car's all he's talked about since he was twelve."

I swallow hard. "I know."

Jackson sees my tears before I feel them. He pulls me up against him, and I burrow into his chest. The song is endless. We wait it out, rocking back and forth, Jackson's cheek resting on top of my head.

I turn so I can see Cody and Brian. They're not dancing anymore, not really, just kind of standing in place, swaying. A few other couples have joined the dancing but keep to the other side of the floor.

"I'm proud of him," Jackson whispers into the top of my head. "Aren't you?"

I swallow down more tears. I don't know why I'm crying, only that the sight of Cody with Brian means everything is different. What if it gets worse for him at school now? Our New York Plan may have to be put into effect sooner rather than later.

"I love him," is what I tell Jackson. "I want him to be happy."

"Me, too."

Finally, the song is over. Brian leads Cody back to our table. Jackson and I join them.

"That must've been some talk," I say to Brian, loudly. The next song is faster, and the dance floor quickly fills up.

I'm ready to go. I am too heavy to dance to the light pop tunes the DJ's playing. But Brian and Cody are deep in conversation. Jenna's across the room at a new table with some other freshman girls. She's careful not to look our way.

Jackson scoots his chair until it bumps into me. "Thanks

for that," he says. "I didn't want him alone out there."

I smile, still fighting back the something in my stomach that won't settle. The something that won't say this is a great thing for Cody. Jackson looks at me and I look back. He's so different since his trip. Quieter. Focused. Kind.

He leans in, all that new quiet focus directed at my lips. Chills break out on my arms just thinking about his kiss. I inch forward in my seat and lift my face toward his.

"Jackson, there you are!" a familiar female voice screeches above the music. "I've been looking everywhere! I stop for one second to adjust my straps, and the next second you're gone!"

I don't want to turn around and see her. I can tell by the stricken look on Jackson's face that I won't like what I see. Cody bought two tickets . . . one for Jackson. And one for Kait.

"Hey," I say, like I wasn't thinking about kissing Jackson five seconds ago. The straps of her blue dress are clearly not up to the task of hefting her nursing-Stephanie breasts. I think there must be some double-stick tape involved.

"What're you doing here?" I knew she wasn't totally in love with Gustavo, that moving in with him was a convenient way to escape our house, our family. But dating Jackson while Gustavo pays her electricity bill? A new low, even for her.

"Abby, it's not what you think," Jackson quickly tries to explain, but I hold up my hand.

"Don't bother," Kait says, no longer looking happy. "Abby's not reasonable."

"*I'm* not—" I'm speechless. "You are a total—" I stand up and fling back the flimsy plastic chair.

"Wait, let me explain." Jackson grabs my arm, but I wrench it away from him.

"Abby!" Jackson yells as I storm off. But I don't turn around, because Rule #4 is blaring in my head. Don't Need Him. Don't Count on Him. Don't think for one second that he needs you.

Chapter ♥ 22

"Abby, wait up!"

It's been less than five minutes since I came outside. The night air is warm and dry, and I'm worried that the sweat I feel building up under my arms will stain my dress. Not that I have anywhere else to wear it, but just in case I find out I'm really the daughter of deposed European royalty, it'd be nice to have the right outfit ready to go.

"Come on, Abby. Let me explain."

I'm such a wimp, I'm actually glad to hear Jackson's voice. But I pretend like I'm not and keep walking.

"Where are you going?" His footsteps are heavy on the ground. He's catching up.

I pick up the hem of my dress and walk faster. I don't know where I'm going. I just know I have to get away from Jackson. Jackson and Kait. Kait and Jackson.

"Abby, it's not what you think!" He's right behind me. His large hand lands on my shoulder and spins me. "Just give me a second here."

"No." I stare at the top button of his shirt, the one directly below the hollow of his collarbone. "No, you don't give me that stupid Rumi poem and then bring my *sister* to the dance and then almost kiss me right in front of her. That's not how it's going to work. That's not who I am."

His hand glides down my arm and circles my wrist. "It's not like that." He tugs a little, but I refuse to look up. "Please, Abby, give me a chance."

I haven't seen Stephanie since Kait took her and moved out almost three weeks ago. I imagine her growing up like Shelby said, looking more and more like Jackson every day. His eyes, his nose, his blond-blond hair.

I force my lips into a smile. "Jackson, it's okay. I get it. You and Kait aren't together now but you've got this, like, lifelong connection through Stephanie. Actually, it's probably better this way. I'm sure you'll be a way better dad than the Guitar Player. But it doesn't matter if you're sleeping with Kait now or not—I won't get tangled up in this. I can't."

Jackson's chin firms up in what I always thought was a Cody-expression of intractability. "I'm not Stephanie's father!" He doesn't shout, but the force behind his words probably carries all the way back to the dance. "Why do you keep saying that? Has Kait said something?"

I shake my head and try to free my wrist from his grasp, but he clamps on. I don't know why I'm so sure he's Stephanie's dad except for the hints Shelby drops every chance she gets. The kicker, though, always comes back to the time line.

"November plus nine months equals Stephanie's birthday in August," I tell him. "There's no getting away from the facts."

"Stephanie was *premature*," Jackson growls. He reaches

out and manacles my other wrist. "Abby, be reasonable."

Reasonable? My breath speeds up like I've been running across the parking lot instead of standing here trying to get Jackson to admit that we are 100 percent over.

"Kait wanted to get the Guitar Player back. That's why she said he's the dad." It's even understandable. Who wants to sit back and watch your ex boyfriend date everyone in your family except you?

Jackson lets go of my wrists and takes a step back. "I can't believe you. This is all Shelby's doing, isn't it? Tell me, if Stephanie's not premature, why did they give Kait special instructions for her care? You think the doctor, the nurses, the hospital—none of them can tell a preemie from a regular newborn? Really?"

"Don't try to wiggle out of this! My family is screwed up enough, and I'm not going to make it worse!" Now that he's released me, I turn and run, high heels and all.

I don't know how long I stumble through the parking lot, Jackson behind me, before I hear Cody calling me. "Abby!" I blink in the sudden impact of his headlights in my eyes. He pulls up beside me. "I'll take you home."

I hop in. Jackson gets smaller and smaller in the rearview mirror. Not that I'm looking.

"Weird night, right?" Cody asks. He's not smiling, but he's not unhappy, either. He's becoming a Cody I don't completely understand. Out. He's really, really out. At least at school, anyway. Jackson, Stephanie, and the whole mess has to take a backseat to what Cody went through tonight.

"What took you so long?" I ask, instead of what I want to know. Which is, why that dance with Brian? Why set himself up for the very thing he's most afraid of?

"As soon as you took off, I came after you. But I got sidetracked."

It must've been something big. He would never leave me stumbling around a dark parking lot, even if the only thing chasing me was his brother. "By who?"

"First Jenna. I had to apologize, right?"

"How'd that go?"

He shakes his head and sighs. "Then Becca stopped me."

"Becca Waters?"

"Yeah, she asked me to dance."

Maybe that dress was a bit tight and cut off the oxygen to her brain. "Not too bright, huh? Didn't she see you with Brian? And what about poor Kent?"

Cody slants a look my way. "I think she just wanted to talk. She asked what I thought about the decorations."

Obsessed much? "That girl is strange."

"She was very insistent."

"I can imagine. What'd you tell her?"

He smiles, big. "Hideous, I told her. What are we, a clown college?"

I laugh, even though five minutes ago I would've said I didn't have it in me. "Did she cry?"

Cody drums his fingers on the steering wheel, fast and erratic. "She asked me to work on the Winter Formal. Said she could really use my input."

Somehow, we're talking about something else, but I'm not

sure what. "You don't care about school dances." That's the Cody I know.

But this Cody says, "I told her I'd be glad to do whatever I could."

There's a long silence. Cody turns onto our street, and my house closes in on us.

"You'll help, too?" he asks as we idle in my driveway. "I kind of already told her you would."

Decorating committees? School dances? What is the world coming to? "Of course I will. You know how I love balloons."

What he really knows is that I'd do anything for him. Even if it means hanging out with Becca-Kent, discussing punch recipes and exactly how long you have to leave sugar cookies out to get the right amount of staleness.

Dad snores. Loudly. I can hear him in the kitchen, where I am sipping a glass of water and wishing it was vodka. The house is dark. I'm still in my princess dress, but I don't feel like a princess. I feel like a rock-'em-sock-'em robot, down for the count.

I wander into the living room and lie down on the couch. The snores bother me from here. Tonight, it seems like too much. I set aside my glass of water and throw an arm over my eyes. Sleep comes quickly.

I wake up with a hand on my breast. Not my hand. Not my bed. A heavy weight anchors me to the couch. The Guitar Player's couch. The Guitar Player's hand.

"Get off!" I wiggle and try to shove him. Not easy with arms pinned.

"Shhh." He presses a kiss to my face. I turn at the last moment, and he misses my lips. Thank God. "Girl, I missed you."

The Guitar Player has been playing a lot of out-of-town gigs. His breath is stale—old beer and cigarettes with just a touch of halitosis. I gag.

"Oh, baby," he croons, and squeezes my breast. "I'm so glad you waited for me."

He thinks I'm Mom. He thinks I was waiting up for him. I open my mouth to correct him and he sticks his tongue in there.

"*Ummfggg,*" is all I can get out. I slap at him.

"Take it easy, Shel," he says into my mouth.

Shel? As in *Shelby*? I'm too stunned to take advantage of his mouth finally leaving mine to cruise down my neck. He makes sucking sounds and I realize, *Oh my God, my sister is sleeping with our stepdad while my mom is pregnant with his baby.* I slap harder.

"Get off me, you creep!" I hiss, wanting to yell but not wanting to wake anyone up. Mom doesn't need to see this. Mom definitely doesn't want to see this. "It's Abby, you numb nuts." For emphasis, I bring up my knee and shove. I hear fabric rip. "Goddamn it, you ripped my dress!" Now I beat on him for real.

"Wha-huh?" Maybe the beer haze is wearing off, because he lets me go like I'm fire and he's made of wood. "Abby?"

"You jerk!" I sit up and punch him in the chest. "Shelby? You're sleeping with Shelby?"

"Shhh." He covers my mouth with his hand. "I was con-fused."

I snort and bite a finger. Hard. He lets go. "I bet. How long? How long have you been cheating on Mom?"

"I don't have to answer to you."

This time I knee him in the nuts for real. "Yes, you do. Because if I don't like what I hear, I'm telling her everything. I'll call the cops and tell them you molested me."

"You wouldn't! It was a mistake!"

"You're the mistake. On second thought, I don't want to hear what you have to say. Get out of this house."

"You can't tell me what to do."

"Get out," I grit out between clenched teeth. "If you know what's good for you, you'll leave and never come back."

He stares at me. I stare back. Let him see how drop-dead serious I am.

"Abby?" Mom's voice breaks the silence. She stands at the opening to the hallway in her boxy pajamas, the ones with the tiny blue-flower print. "What's going on here?"

"The Guitar Player was just leaving," I say. "Right?"

"But you just got here!" Mom flings herself at him and he catches her. Cradles her head in his hands and kisses her mouth.

Gag me. "Mom, listen to me. He—"

"Mona, we have to talk," the Guitar Player says.

Good, he's going to tell her himself. I won't have to be the bad guy.

"What is it, darling?" Mom asks, stroking fingers through his lanky hair. Although she looks like she just woke up, the way she nestles her body against his is anything but sleepy.

He looks at me over her head as he speaks. "Now, don't get mad. Abby kissed me."

"What?" Mom reels back, hand to her heart like an arrow has lodged there. "Abby, how could you?"

"Don't be angry with her. Think she had a little too much to drink tonight. She was so loaded, she couldn't even make it to her room, passed out right here on the couch."

The lying, conniving, evil bastard. "Mom, I haven't had anything to drink! I just crashed here. *He* attacked me while I was asleep! *He* thought I was *Shelby!*"

Her look says more than words. It's like I'm not even her daughter. All she sees is another Guitar Groupie.

"You have to believe me!" I cry. "You know I can't stand him! Why would I do this?"

Mom crosses her arms across her chest. "I don't know, Abby, but I do know you've been against our marriage from the start. I never thought my own daughter would betray me like this, though."

I'm surprised she doesn't choke on the irony. This is exactly what Shelby did to Kait and then what Mom herself turned around and did to Shelby. She's got no room to be self-righteous here.

Mom lays possessive fingers on the Guitar Player's biceps and glares at me. "Don't think you can win this one, Abby. You can't break us up. This is true love right here."

The Guitar Player smirks at me. "That's right, baby."

Me? After *him*? I try to remind her what this fight is really about. "He thought I was Shelby! He's sleeping with Shelby!"

Mom dismisses my words with a wave. "That's in the past. I'm all Steve needs now. Right, honey?"

He nuzzles her hair. "Love you, baby."

Someone kill me now, before I ever act like such an idiot over a guy. Before I'm ever so blind that I sacrifice every last ounce of self-respect for a loser like him. I should thank Kait for going to the dance with Jackson. Although I'd fought it, the truth was I'd started to think Jackson wasn't so bad. That he'd changed enough over the summer to qualify as Someone New. That he really did care about me. Maybe I should even thank the Guitar Player for reminding me at this critical juncture just how slimy men can be.

"I'm going to bed," I announce, smoothing my beautiful, torn dress.

"One second, young lady," Mom says in her Mom voice. "I think you need to apologize."

"I what?" No way. No how.

"Abby, you owe Steve an apology. Now." Steel-voiced, she stares me down.

I smile, first at her, then at him. "I'm sorry you're such a scumbag," I say. "I'm sorry my mom married you. I'm sorry for any child who has to call you 'Dad.'"

Neither one of them speaks. I limp down the hallway on one shoe. I don't know what happened to the other one, but I can't go back in there.

"We'll talk about this in the morning," Mom calls just as I reach my room.

But we don't. In the morning, it's like last night never happened. I'm not the only one in my family who's good at faking amnesia.

Chapter ♥ 23

"He what?" Cody is furious for me. A good thing, since all I can muster up is a faint nausea. He's still in his pajamas—light cotton sweatpants and nothing else—arms crossed against his bare chest. I feel slightly guilty for waking him up when I climbed in his window, but I needed to talk. Besides, it's almost noon. How was I supposed to know he planned to snooze all of Sunday away?

Cody points a finger at me, shaking it like I'm a bad dog. "You've got to tell someone."

Ah, now the shoe's on the other foot, and I suddenly understand why Cody never wanted anyone to know about the incidents at school. Because even though I know it's wrong—that this is all the Guitar Player's fault, that I'm totally blameless—I feel guilty. Also, kind of dirty. No amount of bath scrub's washing away this slime.

"So, are you and Brian a thing now?" Shifting focus, like a scene cut in a soap opera. Very effective for getting out of uncomfortable conversations.

Cody shakes his head. "We're friends, that's all."

"Good friends?" I waggle my eyebrows.

He laughs. "Naw, but he mentioned better sites to check out than the ones I've been surfing."

"Hard to find worse." Really, butt plugs? The bigger question is why supposedly straight, gay-bashing guys would know about them.

"You could try talking to your mom again, now that there's been some time for the shock to wear off." Cody returns to my mini-drama and his bed. He slides under the comforter and fluffs a pillow behind him.

"It was all a stupid mistake," I say, crossing the rug to sit at his desk. I spin the chair to face Cody. "He thought I was Shelby."

"He stuck his tongue in your mouth."

"Shelby wouldn't have minded." What was with my family and the Guitar Player? Was I the only one immune to his scruffy charms?

I should just charge back over to the house and tell Shelby exactly what I think of all this . . . this hanky-panky. But part of me is afraid she'll think the same thing as Mom, and the other part is scared that it'll turn into another Savage-family smackdown. Only this time, it'll be me standing in the driveway putting on a show for the neighbors. Sign me up now, Mr. Springer. No thank you.

"Still . . . " He gives me the look, the one I used to give him about telling on those guys at school.

"Mom knows already. Shouldn't that be enough?" I fiddle with my earring, earlobe, a lock of hair. I can't seem to sit still, so I stand up but then don't know where to go.

"Honey, come here." He holds out his arms and, relieved, I collapse next to him on the bed. He strokes my back and suddenly I'm crying. I turn my head into his neck, stifling my sobs against his smooth skin. I love the way Cody smells. Clean, safe.

"Better?" he asks as I calm down.

I hiccup.

"Because it seems like maybe there's more going on than just what happened with the Guitar Player."

Although Cody was there when Kait showed up, he didn't catch my fight with Jackson in the parking lot. But Cody's watched as much SoapTV as I have, so he plunges right in.

"Is this about Kait and Jackson?" he guesses. "Because there are a million reasonable explanations. He's crazy about *you*, not her."

I'm beginning to really hate the word *reasonable*. I wipe my dribbling nose on Cody's pillow. "No, he's not. Not after last night." I tell Cody that I think Stephanie is really Jackson's and about our argument after the dance.

He doesn't get mad that I didn't tell him about Stephanie sooner, just wraps me in a tight hug and says, "You could've told me you were worried that Jackson was Stephanie's dad. I wouldn't have said anything to him."

"I know." I sniffle into his shirt. "I guess I was afraid to say it out loud. Or that you'd tell me it was true."

"Ah, princess," he says, and runs a hand down my back. "You're crazy sometimes, you know that?"

We're quiet together for a few minutes. I'm almost asleep when he says, "Holy crap, Abs, I might be an uncle!"

✳ ✳ ✳ ✳ ✳

"Abby, you need a girlfriend," Cody says as he fast-forwards through the commercials on Monday's episode of *Passion's Promise*. It's a two-fer Tuesday night—Monday and today together, because we got behind on *Veterans' Hospital* and *Promise*.

We're in my living room, but somehow, he's in charge of the remote. When Cain and Lacey fill the screen, picking up right where they left off under the cream satin sheets, he hits PAUSE.

I glance up from the important work of painting my toe-nails Pistol Packin' Pink. "Just because you've come out of the closet, doesn't mean I'm with you. I mean I'm *with* you, but not *with you*. Definitely into boys here. Wait—you, too, so that means I'm more *with* you than not—"

"Shut up," he says. "I know you're not gay. I'm saying you need a friend-girl, someone to hang with and talk boys and stuff."

The hand holding the nail-polish brush trembles. "That's what you're for, Cody. It's always been you and me."

He shifts position on the couch, crooking one knee toward me. "And it'll always be you and me, but don't you think there's room for some other people, too?"

This isn't about me and girlfriends at all. I click my wet nail against the polish bottle. "Is this about Brian?"

"He mentioned we could use some guy time."

"So is *he* your new best friend or something?" I don't want to sound so hurt. I jam the nail-polish brush back into the bottle.

"No, of course not. It's just . . ."

"What? What aren't you telling me?"

"I feel guilty, okay? Like if Brian and I are hanging out, you should have someone else, too. I don't know how to say it exactly. Like for balance, y'know?"

"It's not that easy," I mumble into my knee, which I have squished up under my chin. "You and Brian have the whole gay thing in common, but who am I supposed to talk to? Can't Brian be my friend, too? We could all hang out, have more movie nights. It's not like I *can't* talk about boys and hair with you guys, right?"

"Yeah, but . . ." Cody sighs, really loud and long, like I'm Hannah and have pulled down my training pants but haven't quite made it to the bathroom in time. "Girl. Friend. Is it really that hard?"

I scrunch myself up tighter. "Have you taken an estrogen-level reading in this house lately? I am drowning in girls here. Why on earth would I go out of my way to find more?"

He laughs, startled. "I hadn't thought of it like that."

"Besides," I say, warming up to my defense, "I have other friends!"

Cody cocks a brow at me. "Really? Name one."

That Kait is the first name that pops into my mind is truly sad, especially since I haven't spoken a word to her since she moved out. Lucas Fielding and I are lab partners, but that's not the same as friends no matter how many times he lets me copy his homework. There are people in all my classes, people I say hi to, but no one I eat lunch with or walk to class with or basically do anything with. This isn't fair. Cody and I have always been best friends. I didn't know I was supposed to have backups.

"See, I'm right." Cody flicks the remote, and Cain and Lacey's moans fill the room. "But you know what? It's fine. I kind of like being the testosterone fix to your over-estrogenated life."

"Yeah, you're the man, all right." I roll my eyes at him and pretend to go back to watching *Promise*. But inside, I'm thinking how I'll show him. I'm going to get a girlfriend, and we'll see how much he thinks it's still such a great idea when I go shopping without him.

I decide that Lucas Fielding should be my new friend-girl. Okay, so he's not a girl, but he's been nice to me in Bio, and I figure he'll make a better girlfriend than Kait would.

It's Wednesday, lab day, and I get to class early. I stack my Bio text and notebook on the black table, line up my pencils and pens exactly so, and wait for Lucas.

He comes in by himself. Bonus! He clearly needs a new friend, too. I smile really big at him and motion for him to come sit by me. Which he has to do anyway, since we're lab partners and all.

"Hey!" I say too loudly. "How'd the homework go last night?"

He rummages through his binder, brown bangs sweeping in to cover his hazel eyes. Bonus! His eyes are almost the same color as Cody's. That should make it easy to be friends, right?

"Did you need to copy?" he asks, handing me a few sheets

of notebook paper covered in hand-drawn genetic tables.

"No, no. Look, I did my own." I get out my tables, which are less neat than his, to show him.

His eyes graze my paper, and then his face goes blank.

"What?"

"It's, um, good that you did it all on your own." He flushes.

I look at my notes, then look at his. "You might as well tell me."

"It's fine," he says. "Nothing big."

I study the homework more carefully, then see what he saw at first glance. I grab my pencil and erase furiously, correcting my chart so that the baby does not end up with sickle-cell disease. Nothing I can do about the color-blindness without redoing the whole thing. Poor little guy won't get to be an interior decorator when he grows up.

"Thanks," I say. "You're a good friend." Because saying it makes it true, right?

He flushes an even deeper red but doesn't respond, because Mr. Kimball comes in from his secret office—a connective space between the classroom and the lab that's he squeezed a small desk into—and thumps on one of the lab tables.

"Listen up. Today we're doing a very dangerous and thrilling lab." He wiggles his fingers like a magician. "A lab so ancient, so barbaric, that our very own school board once outlawed it."

Everyone who was talking stops.

"A lab that involves blood sacrifice." He stops and looks around the room. "A lab that involves"—he pulls a small lancet from the pocket of his gray slacks—"sharp, pointy things!"

Lucas and I look at each other. He shrugs and raises his hand. "Will this be on the AP test?"

Mr. Kimball visibly deflates. "Mr. Kimball, the all-powerful, does not know every question on the AP exam. That would be cheating. Mr. Kimball assures you, yet again, Mr. Fielding, that everything we do will prepare you for the big test.

"Any other questions?" Mr. Kimball lays the lancet on the table and shoves his hands in his pockets.

"Um?" Veronica Ortega raises her hand. "What exactly are we doing?"

Mr. Kimball explains that we're going to figure out our own blood types, which seems pretty cool to me. We've been making charts for imaginary offspring of insects, mammals, and even humans, but now we're doing something real.

"This lab was very common back when I started teaching, but the AIDS scare in the eighties brought up the issue of safety. Let me assure you this lab is completely safe. We'll be taking precautions—using gloves, everyone working with only their own blood, following my directions *exactly*—and of course, anyone who doesn't want to participate in this lab may opt out and do an outline of chapter three instead. Are we clear?"

I nod my head and I guess everyone else does, too, because he starts passing out kits. I open mine and find hospital-like gloves, a lancet, microscope slides, and an alcohol pad. Mr. Kimball calls our attention to the front and demonstrates how to prick your finger—swab first!—and how to get the blood onto the slide. "Remember, no partners today. Everyone's on their own."

"Excuse me?" Veronica doesn't raise her hand this time, but the lab's so quiet that Mr. Kimball turns to her right away.

"Yes?" He adjusts the microscope on the front table.

"If it was banned and stuff, why are we doing this?"

Mr. Kimball frowns and turns to face the class. "If you don't want to do it, you don't have to. The thing is, this particular lab is special to me. Back in my day, when dinosaurs roamed the earth and Adam and Eve were my neighbors, science class was all about read the chapter, answer the questions, take a test. Then, one day, my Biology teacher had us do this lab. And when I looked under the scope and saw my own blood and was able to figure out I was type-B all by myself, well, I thought, *Science is cool.* Besides, as AP students, I thought you'd be up for the challenge."

Veronica looks at her finger and the lancet, and says, "I'll be outlining chapter three, if that's okay?"

Poor Mr. Kimball. Even though I'm not exactly thrilled to prick my own finger, I close my eyes and jab.

"Ow! Oh my God." Perhaps I've jabbed too hard. Blood drips from my fingertip. Without thinking, I bring it to my mouth and suck. The bleeding stops.

"Ms. Savage? You okay?" Mr. Kimball is behind me, his coffee-flavored breath spreading over my workstation.

I take the finger out of my mouth. "Pretty dumb, huh? Now I'm going to have to do it again."

He pats my back and walks away. "You'll be okay. Remember you have a little over three liters of blood in your body. A few drops won't kill you."

Comforting. My poor abused finger. I decide to sacrifice a different one this time. Close my eyes and . . .

"Abby?" It's Lucas, his one eye looking at me and the other one focused a little beyond my right ear.

I place my lancet on the table. "What?"

He holds out his own lancet and extends the one hand that is not gloved. "Will you do it for me?"

Turning my head, I track down Mr. Kimball in the back row, helping Shauna get her slide under the microscope. "We're not supposed to."

Lucas swallows, his Adam's apple bobbing like a yo-yo. "I can't do it. Please."

"Fine." I double-check Mr. Kimball's whereabouts and say, "Close your eyes."

He does. I take his lancet and put it in his right hand. Holding his left, I say, "Okay, I'm going to help you. Ready?"

"Did you do it yet?" He opens one eye.

"Keep 'em closed! And listen. When I say three, push down hard." I guide the lancet into position, then let go. "One, two, three, jab!" A tiny pinprick of blood bubbles to the surface of his skin. "You did it! Let's get your slide."

Lucas and I set up his slide and get it under the microscope. "This is so cool," he says. "Look!"

I push my eyelashes against the viewer. Lucas's blood is right there, and you can actually see the individual cells. "That's so cool."

Now I'm really anxious to get mine done. I use the same pressure as I did on Lucas's hand, and I also get a small bubble.

I quick get my slide ready and then study my own blood.

"Lucas?" I distract him from his slide. "How do we tell what kind of blood we have?"

He takes over my scope and has a look. "You've got to add the solution." He flags down Mr. Kimball, who puts a small drop of reagent on my slide.

"I started with the anti-A reagent," Mr. Kimball says. "Check your scope. Do you see clumping?"

"Yep," I nod.

"Lucky on the first try!" Mr. Kimball crows. "You're an A."

"Does that mean I get an A?" I ask. He chuckles and walks away.

I fill out my worksheet and ask Lucas, "What're you?"

"AB." He fills out his own lab report. "If we had a kid, their blood would most likely be a B."

Whoa, kids? Maybe I've been too friendly today. "You can really tell what kind of blood your child will have?"

He shrugs one shoulder. "Sure, it's just like the genetic tables we did for homework last night. If you know two of the blood types, you should be able to figure out the third."

I get an idea. A great idea. "Does it work in reverse? Like if you know the baby and the mom, can you tell what blood type the father has?"

He stops writing and taps his pencil on the table. "I don't see why not. I mean, it wouldn't be infallible, but you could take a pretty good guess." He opens his Bio book and flips to the back. "Here, they've even got tables you could use to help you figure it out."

Oh my gosh, this is better than Cain and Lacey finally getting together on *Passion's Promise*. And bonus! I may even get extra credit for finally figuring out who Stephanie's dad really is.

"Thanks, Lucas!" I say, and almost ask him if he wants to eat lunch with me. But then I remember our kids and think it's better if we just stay lab partners.

It's not as easy to casually work blood types into a conversation as you might think, especially when you're not talking to one of the people whose blood type you most need to know.

"Shelby?" I knock on the door to her room and then push it open. Mom's suitcase, the one so old it doesn't even have wheels, is opened up on Shelby's bed. There are a few pairs of underwear in the inside mesh pocket. She's folding her silky pajama bottoms. "Going somewhere?"

Shelby jumps like she's surprised it's me. "No, not really. Just another weekend away."

With Dean, no doubt. He must have beaucoup bucks. "I can't babysit this weekend." I try to head her off.

She just smiles and says, "Don't worry. Dad said he'd take care of her."

"Oh, good." I sit on the bed. Shelby tosses me her jeans, and I obediently fold them and place them in the suitcase. "Can I ask you something?"

"Sure, as long as you keep folding." She takes a drawer of T-shirts and tanks and dumps them on my lap.

"You ever have Kimball for science?"

"Yeah, sure. He's been there forever."

"Did you have to type your blood?"

Shelby's rolling socks but stops to look at me. "Yep. It was pretty cool. That why you've got a Band-Aid on two fingers? Labs must still be on Wednesdays."

I smile at her. "I jabbed a little too hard the first time. I found out my blood type's A. Do you remember yours?"

"Sure, A, like you. Why, you looking for a donor or something? Got an incurable disease?" She laughs and tosses a sock ball at me. I deflect it into the suitcase with an upraised hand.

My brain pedals fast for some kind of explanation that does not involve Jackson and Stephanie. "Just worrying about Hannah. With you going out of town so much lately, what if something happens? We should know her blood type, don't you think?"

Shelby laughs. "I remember Mr. Kimball getting us all worried about bleeding out at the hospital because no one knew our blood type. Hannah's a B, like her dad." Whenever Shelby speaks of He-Who-Divorced-Her, she gets a faraway look in her eye.

I feel like Nancy Drew, all detective-y and stuff, when I say, "Is there anyone in our family who's the same type?" Like Kait? I want to prompt, but let her answer in her own way.

"Yeah," she says, long hair swishing as she walks across the room to get the body mist off her dresser. "Kait and Mom are both A. I remember, because I bled a lot when Hannah was born and almost had to have a blood transfusion. They were candidates. But then the doctor got the bleeding to stop, and I didn't need one after all."

"What if Hannah needs blood and the hospital's out of B? Wouldn't that be a disaster?"

"Overreact much?" Shelby chews her lip while deciding which pair of skanky heels to pack—red stilettos or black wedges with ankle wraps? "But I think Steve could probably be a donor. Once, when we were dating, we were gonna donate blood. You know, for the money? But after answering, like, a bazillion questions, we found out that they don't give you anything but a cookie afterwards. So we blew that place, but I remember seeing his form, and he was a B like Hannah."

Bonus! Who knew Shelby would be such a font of bloody wisdom? She's solved half my mystery without even knowing it.

"Cool," is all I say. I watch as Shelby packs some barely-there bras. "Can I ask you something else?" Since she's being so helpful and all, I figure why not take one more shot in the dark?

"Shoot," she says.

"Are you still sleeping with *him*?" I thought I could let it go, fake amnesia like the rest of my family, but sometimes, when I'm not thinking about anything else, I think about that. How my dress got ripped and *his* tongue in my mouth. Not that I'm doing anything about it, it'd just be nice to know.

The sock ball she throws at me this time is no joke. It bounces off my shoulder with enough force to remind me that she played softball for a whole lotta years. "God, Abby. Do you have to be so awful?"

Which I guess is as close to a "no" as I'll get from her, be cause she clams up and stomps off to the bathroom.

I stay on her bed, inspecting the contents of her bag. I should've known the Guitar Player was lying. Have I learned nothing from my family? Men lie, and when they get caught, they lie some more.

Chapter ♥ 24

Some people would be thrilled that their parents were back together. I am merely thrilled that Dad is moving out of my bedroom. But the fact that he's only moving down the hall, into the bed so recently vacated by the Guitar Player, is not thrilling.

"He really was sleeping with Shelby all along," Mom cries into my shoulder. Does she apologize for doubting me? No, she does not.

We are standing in the driveway on Saturday morning as Shelby and the Guitar Player drive away together. I don't know how I feel. Relieved. He's gone and hopefully it's for good. Mad. Can Shelby not see what a loser he is? Was there ever really a Dean or was it the Guitar Player all along? And how dare she trick me into helping her pack?

"She'll be back," Dad says, coming up behind us. He was the only one who didn't seem that surprised when Shelby made her announcement on Thursday night. He even paid for a motel for her since things were so "awkward" at home.

"It takes some people longer than others to get over fools' mountain."

Now that he is in Dad mode again, he's started spouting random bits of his life's philosophy at us. But I hope he's right. I hope Shelby does come back, especially if she's ditched the Guitar Player by then. If not for her sake, then for Hannah's. I'm glad I'm not the one who has to tell her Mommy's gone, but don't worry, Grandma will be your new mom for now. Of course, it could be worse. The Guitar Player and Shelby could've taken Hannah with them. Who knows how much the therapy to recover from that kind of damage would cost?

We go back in the house. Hannah is watching cartoons. It seems like a good way to spend the afternoon. Only there's no couch—because the Guitar Player trashed it in a rather impressive show of infantile rage when Mom said leaving it was the least he owed her—so I snuggle with Hannah on a big pillow and let Mom have the Barcalounger. She tosses me a blanket. It's like we're all being careful of each other. Like we're afraid of breaking something. But I think we're too late. I think it's already broken.

"Abby, get dressed." Cody shakes me awake on Sunday afternoon. "It's three o'clock. You have to get up."

I've been sleeping a lot since Dad moved down the hall. It's awfully peaceful having my own room. I stretch and Cody steps back. "Whoa, honey, you need a shower."

I frown but stumble to the bathroom. When I'm clean and wearing the jeans and green halter top Cody chose while I was showering, he sits me down on the bed. "We need to talk."

"Did Walt take your car again?" It's the only thing I can think of that would crinkle his forehead like that.

"No, it's about Jackson."

I wave my hand at him. "I'm not talking about him. Let's pick someone else from your list. Andre didn't work out, but there are still plenty more guys to go through. Hey, maybe I'll even find one for you." I wink at him.

Cody grinds his teeth. "I'm being serious."

"Okay, what about Jackson?"

"He's going back to Nicaragua."

"I know."

"You know? How?" Cody folds his arms across his chest.

"He told me. It's, like, his dream."

"He's leaving tonight. Tonight, Abby." Cody thumps one foot like an impatient teacher waiting for a slow kid to spit out an answer.

"Tonight?" I echo, like I am that slow kid. "How long have you known?"

"There was something on the news about an earthquake in the area where he worked. He made a few phone calls yester-day, and now it's bye-bye U.S.A."

Of course he'd go. They need him, and after a disaster, they'd need him even more.

"Your parents bought him a ticket?" I remember that they cut off his college money, and as far as I know, hanging out at home doesn't pay well.

"Sold his car to one of his friends. Can you believe it?"

Of course I can, but that doesn't explain why I suddenly can't catch my breath.

Thump, thump, goes Cody's sandal on the wood floor. "Abigail Elizabeth Savage, do you really want him to go without saying good-bye?"

Tears well in my eyes. I ignore them and shrug. "We said everything we needed to say at homecoming."

Cody sighs and reaches into his pocket. "He told me to give you this." It's a folded note. He flings it at me and leaves.

It sits on the bed next to me. Finally, I open it. More Rumi. Sad Rumi, about how effort doesn't matter. Either love is or is not.

Underneath, he wrote, *Abby, I give up.*

I can't stop crying.

"Take me to Kait's."

It's evening. Mom and Dad are in the kitchen, sharing a glass of wine. Hannah's under the table with the whisk in her mouth.

"Now?" Mom takes a sip. "Why now?"

Because I've finally stopped crying and I need to know the truth. It would've been so easy to ask Kait at the dance, or call her, or respond to Jackson's first note. But I didn't. And now it might be too late. To Mom I say, "Will you take me? I really need to talk to Kait."

"That's funny," Dad says. "She called yesterday and asked for you."

"She did?"

"Didn't I tell you?" He looks confused and it irritates me. Is it so hard to write down a message?

"Please?" I use my begging voice. "Please, Mom, I need you to take me."

"I'll take you," Dad says.

I ignore him. It would be safer to go with him, but this is a girl thing. "Mom?"

She sighs and sets down her glass. "I'm not supposed to be drinking this anyway. Let me get my purse."

Gustavo lives in a nicer part of town than we do, in a cute little condo building closer to the tourist trap that is Old Town. I fidget while Mom rings the doorbell.

"Mom!" Kait looks surprised. She has Stephanie in the baby sling around her neck. "Abby? Come in!"

The condo is immaculate, white tile floors and white furniture with shaggy black pillows. There's a huge TV on the wall with the most enormous DVD collection I've ever seen, housed on simple black shelves. I walk closer and see that the DVDs are in alphabetical order. Cody would so approve. Since our room was never clean, I don't think for a minute it's Kait's work we're seeing.

Kait ushers us into the living room and settles Stephanie into a baby swing that is set up in the corner. It's hard to believe I haven't seen her in almost a month, and even harder to take is that fact that she's grown so much. Her eyebrows have darkened, and her tiny, tiny feet aren't quite as little anymore.

"You came for a visit?" Kait asks, planting herself on the couch.

"What, you thought you'd never see us again?" I sound cranky, and it's because I know I should've called or come over sooner. Stephanie shouldn't be growing up without Aunt Abby around. Mom takes a seat on the opposite end of the couch from Kait while I pace between the baby swing and shelves.

"I was beginning to wonder." Kait twirls a strand of hair around her finger, and I notice she's added some dark honey-colored highlights. It looks good. I almost tell her so, but then she says, "So why are you here?"

I decide to plunge in. "It's about Jackson."

"I knew it!" Mom crows. Kait gives her a weird look.

"We're just friends," Kait says. "If you'd stuck around at homecoming, I would've told you. Gustavo was supposed to take me, but his assistant manager got the flu and no one else could work at the store. I didn't want to go alone—I mean, I'm not a total loser. . . ."

"So you used his second ticket?" I ask, wanting to get this perfectly clear.

Kait shakes her head, and the new highlights glint as her hair swings. "I had my own, but Jackson told me he had an extra because Trey enlisted this summer and got sent to North Carolina last week for boot camp."

Just like Cody'd said. A perfectly *reasonable* explanation. Trey and Jackson had been on the football team together for years and were good friends, but midway through their senior year, Trey moved to Flagstaff. Of course Jackson would buy an extra ticket so he could come. Mom reaches over, takes my hand, and squeezes.

"Really?" I ask. "For real, just friends? No games, no flirting? No lifelong connection?" I glance Stephanie's way, but Kait misses my meaning.

Kait smiles at me, big. Holds out her left hand. "I'm about to become Kaitlyn Mercado. There's no way I'm messing that up." The ring on her finger glitters in the light.

"Is it real?" Mom asks, which is not the right response.

"Wow, congratulations!" I say, and hug her. "I had no idea."

Kait's smile gets bigger, if that's possible. "Gustavo loves me. Really loves me. And Stephanie, too. You'll be my maid of honor, right? That's what I called about yesterday. I was worried when you didn't call back."

"Of course!" I say, already thinking about how my princess dress will make a fine maid-of-honor gown once the tear is fixed. "I'm so happy for you. You love him, too, right?"

Kait makes her patented you're-such-a-freak face at me. "Duh! Plus Dr. Patty says that children raised in an intact family unit are less likely to become delinquent or involved in crime as teens. So of course I said yes when Gustavo asked me to marry him! I don't want Stephanie to grow up and be a klepto or a murderer or something."

Mom is still examining the ring. "It looks real."

Kait snatches back her hand. "It is! Jeez, Mom."

"I'm just looking out for you," Mom says. "A fake diamond is no sign of commitment."

Stephanie gets fussy in her swing. Mom puts up a hand. "I've got it." She hurries over and picks up her granddaughter. "Hi there, sweetie. What's wrong?" Then she degenerates into baby coo and walks with Stephanie into the kitchen.

Kait watches until they're out of sight. "Think I should worry?"

I sit on the couch next to Kait. "She raised us." Which is not reassuring, come to think of it.

Kait bites her lip and says, "She's better lately, don't you think? Like something changed."

"Like her daughter ran off with her husband? That's a big change."

"At first, when she called me, I was so shocked. I mean, Mom always gets what she wants. It's like she's been charmed her whole life." Kait worries the lip between her teeth. "But I was reading this other book, *I'm Doing My Best!: Single Mothers Speak Out*, and this one mom talked about how having a baby when she was sixteen made her feel cheated. She missed out on what everyone else her age was doing and had this huge responsibility. I never thought of Mom like that, but it's kind of what happened to her, right?"

I'm glad that Dr. Patty is not Kait's only source of psychobabble, and what she's saying kind of makes sense. "I guess. Mom's never made it a secret that we definitely cramp her style."

"But for all that, she does love us," Kait says. "Now that I have Stephanie, I get that. It doesn't matter about the special feedings and the lack of sleep or the extra trips to the doctor that, thank God, Gustavo is paying for. She's everything to me. Mom must've felt that for us, don't you think?"

"She's good at hiding it," I say. "But maybe."

"Look at Shelby. She just left Hannah behind. Mom never abandoned us. That's something, I think. And now that she's older, she'll probably be a better mom to the new baby. Dr. Patty says older parents tend to be more relaxed."

"You seem pretty good with the whole mom thing." I curl a foot underneath me and shift one of the shaggy pillows onto my lap. "Almost like an expert."

She laughs. "Maybe someday!"

Then I remember the other thing I need cleared up. I decide to ease into the subject. "Hey, Kait, it doesn't bother Gustavo that Stephanie's not his?"

"She is."

I must look shocked, because Kait rushes to explain. "That's what he says. She's his in all the ways that matter."

"Ah, that's sweet." I clutch and unclutch the pillow. "So, he's not jealous of Stephanie's real dad?"

Kait laughs again. "I can't believe I ever thought I loved Steve. Gustavo is good to me, Abby. He doesn't have anything to be jealous of."

I can't outright accuse of her lying. Plan B goes into action. "You wouldn't happen to know Stephanie's blood type, would you?"

"Why? You sick or something?" she asks with what might be real concern on her face.

"No." I scramble for a not-crazy-sounding reason. "What if I'm babysitting for you and . . . "

Kait squeals and hugs me. "You'll babysit? Oh my God, that's so great."

Untangling myself from her arms, I say, ". . . and there's some kind of accident and she needs blood . . . ?"

Leaning back on the cushions, Kait smiles. "Did you just

do Mr. Kimball's blood-typing thingy? Because I was so paranoid after his whole talk about people dying because they got the wrong kind of blood transfusion and—"

"Sheesh, Kait, just answer the question."

She's puzzled and then brightens. "Stephanie's a B—that's what the paperwork from the hospital said."

I hug her again and wonder how long it will take us to get back home. If Shelby's right, the Guitar Player is a B and that makes it possible he really is Stephanie's biological dad. And right now, with Kait so shiny and happy and Stephanie with her new dad, Jackson's blood type doesn't seem that important. There's really only one thing I need to say to him, and that I definitely have do in person.

Mom returns from the kitchen and hands off Stephanie to Kait. "We all done?" she asks with a look that makes me think maybe she heard every word we said.

I kiss my niece good-bye and my sister, too. Mom hurries to the car, but I'm afraid no matter how fast we go, I'm going to be too late.

"Can't we go any faster?"

It normally doesn't take longer going one way across town than the other, but Mom has managed to turn onto a street with major construction. It's evening, which means there shouldn't be bulldozers out scooping up loads of sand and then blocking traffic as they *putt-putt-putt* at three miles an hour to the dump site, but there's at least one and it's caused a backup several miles long. One side of the road is ripped up. We're trapped on the other, crawling along. The Benz wheezes, but we've gotten used to the sound. We pull to a stop, then inch forward again. I am *dying*. And she knows it.

"Don't worry, Abby, there's plenty of time." She turns to look at me.

I look out the window. "Mom!"

"What?" Her reflexes are bad. She hits the accelerator instead of the brakes. We come within millimeters of ramming the car in front of us. She realizes her mistake and jerks the wheel to the side. Faster than a blink, we're in the construction ditch. The Benz wheezes, then chokes. The engine dies. She turns the key and nothing happens.

"Oh, crap," she says.

Chapter ♥ 25

I may have gotten the Rules wrong. There might be something more important than being safe. Driving down I-17 in Cody's car as he rehearses for a career in NASCAR certainly tests that theory. Because a sane person would point out that driving twenty or thirty miles over the speed limit is dangerous, but I don't have time to be cautious. Jackson's plane is scheduled to leave in two hours. It seems like plenty of time, but too much has gone wrong today to count on any good luck.

The Benz had to be towed. Dad came to get us, chuckling at the mess Mom had gotten us into now. Has no one thought of taking this woman's license away from her? Dad insisted Mom go to the emergency room to make sure the baby was okay. Since we'd hit speed bumps harder than we'd hit the ditch, I wasn't worried about her. Dad dropped me at home, where I'd immediately gone next door to beg Cody for a ride.

Of course, Cody came through. He printed out a map, so we'd know where to park and which direction I should run when we finally got to the Phoenix Sky Harbor, which is just an airport, although it sounds like some kind of interstellar refueling station.

Cody's cell phone rings, that annoying disco song he knows I hate. Both his hands are on the wheel and he needs his concentration, so I wrangle it out of his side pocket and say, "Hello?"

"Oh, Abby!" It's Mom, and she's crying. "Barbara said you were with Cody, and I really needed to get ahold of you. . . ."

"What happened?" I'm frantic because if something's wrong, how can we turn around when it's taken me so long to figure out what I want?

"It's a girl!" she sobs into the phone. "They did a sonogram in the ER, and the baby's a girl!"

Okay, this is not call-me-in-a-panic news, but I have to make allowances for hormones. "That's great," I say.

"I know! I'm so happy!" She cries harder. I actually hear the snot build up.

"Can you put Dad on?"

"Hey, pumpkin," he answers. "Your mom's agreed to marry me again! You know, as soon as both our divorces are final. Great news, isn't it?"

Oh, Jesus. I brace my feet on the glove compartment. "Yeah, I guess. What about the baby? It doesn't matter that she's not, you know, yours?"

He laughs into the phone. "Well, it's not totally impossible that she's not."

So much more info than I needed right now. "Uh, great then. Congrats." I flip the phone shut and hold it in my lap.

"Oh my God," Cody says, clearly having heard it all. Really, there's nothing else to say. We're quiet for a long stretch of road until we hit the airport.

"Just go!" Cody drops me off at Departures. "I'll catch up after I park."

Have I mentioned that Cody is the best friend in the universe?

My canvas tote bangs against my side as I run past the ticketing counters, toward the security area closest to his gate. In my mind, I see how this will play out. It'll be just like the time Leah from *Moments of Our Lives* had a psychic vision that Duke's plane to Washington, D.C., was going to crash and she had to rush to the airport to stop him.

I'll run up the down escalators toward the gate. Jackson, looking rugged in his backpacking gear, will have just heard his flight called. He'll rise from his seat, pulling the plane ticket out of his back pocket. He'll hand it to the stewardess, smiling his great smile at her. I'll run, but not fast enough.

"Jackson!" I'll yell, and although lots of people will turn to look at me, *he* won't. He'll walk through the door, onto the skyway, and disappear from my life forever.

Duke never did come back to the show. Hard to when your body's supposed to be scattered in tiny bits across the Atlantic.

Or maybe it'll be more like the *Veterans' Hospital* ending, when Malibu had to stop Paul from taking that ambassador's position in Europe.

"Jackson!" I'll yell, running in his direction. "Jackson, don't leave me!"

He'll turn. Do a double-take. Rip the ticket out of the flight attendant's hand and run toward me. We'll meet up under a display board.

"Abby! You came!" he'll say, covering my face in kisses.

"My darling, I couldn't let you go," I'll say.

"I didn't want to go," he'll reply. "I only left because I thought you wanted me to."

"No, never!" We'll kiss, large and sloppy. "I can't live without you."

"And I can't live without you!" More kissing.

The flight attendant will tap his shoulder. "Excuse me, sir. Your flight's about to leave. You really need to get on that plane."

"I'm not going anywhere," he'll say. Then he'll rip his ticket in two and fling the pieces behind him. "I'm never going anywhere without you again."

Cut to the bedroom scene, the candles, and the satin sheets. And we'll live happily ever after.

Unfortunately, reality is turning out way different. Yes, I'm running through the airport terminal like a crazy person. Yes, I'm yelling "Jackson!" because I can see him up ahead. But there's still an hour until his flight leaves and the line he's standing in is for the metal detector. The security guard watches me like this is the most interesting thing he's seen all day. In fact, a lot of people are watching, but I push them out of my mind. I have to focus here.

"Jackson!"

"Abby?" He looks surprised. Well, he should be surprised after the things I said to him. Or didn't say. He steps out of the line and walks toward me. *Walks.* I slow down.

"Jackson," I pant, catching my breath. "I have to talk to you."

"Yeah, I get that." He guides me over to an empty alcove by a door that says NO ADMITTANCE. He drops his oversized backpack between us on the ground and leans against the door. "What's up?"

He looks at me and I look at him. This is the moment. I have to choose. Stay safe, use the Rules, stick to the Plan. Or go for what I really want, who I really want, and find a way to make it work.

"I love you," I say, watching him closely.

His back straightens. He kicks his backpack to the side. His hands grip my shoulders, and he pulls me closer to him. "You what?"

"I love you."

"You're telling me *now*?"

Okay, I never thought about that part. That he might be mad at me for waiting too long. Maybe I've screwed things up past fixing.

"Um, yeah? Because, well, I kind of wanted to tell you in person. Not, like, in the airport, but you're leaving and I just figured it out."

"Just figured it out?" His hands cup the back of my neck. "When?"

I look at my watch. "Couple hours?"

"And it took you this long to tell me?" He smiles and lowers his head. Our lips meet, his teasing and light, and I can finally breathe. It's going to be okay.

"I'm not too late?" I ask after a few minutes of spit swapping. "You're not mad?"

He wraps me in his arms and holds me close to him. "Your timing does kind of suck. You know I'm leaving the country, right?"

"I *was* running," I remind him.

"But lucky for you, I'll be back in a few months."

"You will?" I jump a little, rubbing our fronts together. "I thought you were going for good."

"I was." He smoothes down my hair. "But Mom got to me with all this talk of how much more help I'd be as a doctor or at least some kind of social worker. That, hey, there're needy kids right here in our own country, too. So I talked to the A.U. people. They've deferred my enrollment until spring term. I'll be home by Christmas."

I'm so happy, all I can do is kiss him. Then something occurs to me.

"Hey, does Cody know this?"

"Of course. We had a big family powwow last night."

That little . . .

Of course his leaving out certain critical facts did lead to this very nice moment. "He's sneaky," is all I say.

Jackson squeezes me hard. "I can't believe you finally say you love me and we're at an airport. And I have to leave. When I get back, Abby, I expect you to be waiting for me. Here. You're the first thing I want to see when I get off the plane."

I look at the big security sign a few feet away. "After your luggage?"

"Whatever. Just promise you'll be here for me."

"What's in it for me?"

He laughs. "I'll show you." And then he kisses me like there's nothing else in the world more important to him than getting as close to me as possible. It could be addictive, this kind of kiss. But I decide it's okay. Jackson won't let me down.

"Jackson?"

"Hmmm?"

"Is there something you want to tell me? About how you feel, maybe?"

"First, you tell me. What about your Rules?"

"What Rules?" I bat my eyelashes at him. "I have no idea what you're talking about. But I do have a quick question for you, just out of curiosity."

"Go ahead." He kisses down the side of my throat, making it kind of hard to remember what I was going to ask.

"Uh, you don't happen to know your blood type, do you?"

He pulls back enough to give me a strange look. "Sure, it's one of the reasons I'm in such a rush to get to Nicaragua. A lot of people were injured in that earthquake, and they need blood. I'm an O-negative."

Which makes him a universal donor, and a statistically improbable father for Stephanie. Not that it matters to me anymore, but it is nice to know. "That's perfect!" I laugh, thinking how sometimes following your heart is way better than following Rules.

Jackson puts a finger under my chin and lifts my face to his. "I love you, Abby Savage. Promise you'll wait for me."

It's an easy promise to make, because one thing I've learned from soap operas is that once you find True Love, you should never, ever let go.

Acknowledgments ♥

So many generous and talented people helped make this book a reality. I'd like to extend special thanks to:

Michael Crumpton, my husband, who listens and listens and listens and never stops believing. . . .

Herman Geerling, my dad, who made a lot of sacrifices so I could have such a nice life. Thank you for teaching me that the difference between winning and losing is *this* much.

Alexandra Flinn and Joyce Sweeney, mentors and friends, without whom I'd never have gotten this far.

Laurie Calkhoven, who keeps me writing even when I don't want to.

Olimpia Reyes, who always puts others before herself. Thank you for easing my burdens. *T'amo.*

Hank and Pat Geerling for helping with the initial research and for your many and great kindnesses to my parents.

Debbie De Leon and Dr. Rollo De Leon, for your generosity and ability to answer all questions about babies.

George Nicholson, for not giving up. Thank you.

Joy Peskin, who is both brilliant and kind. Thank you for taking a chance.

* * * * *

Thank you to Joyce's Thursday night group, especially—
Deborah Sharp, Heidi Boehringer, Kathy MacDonald, Kingsley
Guy, Gale Payne, Stel Fine, Dorian Cirrone, Mel Taylor, Ellyn
Laub, and Lucille Shulklapper. Thank you for sharing so much
with me.

To my Florida SCBWI friends who have supported me
every step of the way, especially—Linda Bernfeld, Adrienne
Sylver, Danielle Joseph, Gaby Triana, Liz Trotta, Meaghan Sylver,
Saundra Rubiera, Stacy Davids, Norma Davids, Steven dos
Santos, Angela Padron, Ellen Slane, Pascale MacAuley, Susan
Shamon, and Elaine Landau.

* * * * *

A heartfelt thank-you to the Viking staff who have been so
generous with their time and talents, especially Regina Hayes,
Kendra Levin, Nico Medina, Christian Fünfhausen, and
Nancy Brennan. There aren't enough words to thank the
people who make a dream come true!